SHADOW GIRL

LINDA RUTH BROOKS

GUM TREE
press

NATIONAL
LIBRARY OF AUSTRALIA

A catalogue record for this
book is available from the
National Library of Australia

Fiction/social issues/contemporary romance

Cover, text design and typesetting & interior design by Linda Ruth Brooks

ISBN: 978-1-7642121-6-8
978-0-6455650-4-1; 978-0-6450817-8-7

Shadow Girl and other books by Linda Brooks, may be purchased through online
bookstores and retail outlets

Author

Linda Brooks lives in Adelaide. She writes nonfiction, poetry, fiction and short stories. She has published and illustrated children's books.

Linda completed a BA Hons in Creative Writing from Southern Cross University (2019). She gained a publisher for her childhood memoir *A Curious & Inelegant Childhood*. She has written a nonfiction book on living with Asperger's Syndrome (autism spectrum) *I'm not broken, I'm just different* and the children's book *Callan the Chameleon* with contributions from Professor Tony Attwood.

Published in anthologies: *Coastlines 5, 6, 7 & 8* by Southern Cross University; *Wood, Bricks & Stone,* Catchfire Press; *Grieve,* Newcastle Writers Centre; *Third Wednesday Poets*; *Seeking the Sun,* Central Coast Poets; *Times Past* Stringybark Press and *Longing for Solitude.*

Awards: Rebecca Coyle Scholarship for Hons; first prize for Legacy University Level Creative Writing Award; first prize in the Gabe Reynaud Creative Writing Award and the Mater Misericordiae Grieve Writing Award.

A registered nurse and advocate for disability in a previous life, Linda has a rich background in listening to the stories of others, never shying away from the darker, gritty tales. And yet, humour is never far away. Linda enjoys hearing from her readers:

lindaruthbrooks@bigpond.com

Author titles

Nonfiction:
I'm not broken, I'm just different
(on Asperger's with Professor Tony Attwood)
A Curious and Inelegant Childhood

Adult fiction:
Behind Whispering Hands
Butterfly Pinning
The Unprize
A broken hallelujah
Scarlett doesn't live here anymore
Under the Bracken Fern

Children's books:
A Tabby Never Forgets
Callan the Chameleon (Asperger's Syndrome)
Dusty Bunny's Very Important Job
Izzy & Pudding the Cat
I want a monkey!
Madam Iris Bigglesworth
The Banyula Tales - 6 stories
Who Stole Christmas?

Publisher of the anthologies:
We are Australian'
The Great Australian Shed
Waltzing Matilda

For Shantel
Beauty & bravery

Contents

Waiting...

A heavy morning fog draped the Onkaparinga hills with thick white mist that crept into corners, flowed down winding roads to the seaside village of Noarlunga. Even the animals sought shelter, unable to see beyond their noses. Winter chills swirled and seeped into bones old and young. Heavy nimbus clouds, anxious to greet the day hovered on the horizon.

On a narrow, potted dirt road halfway to the valley a slender woman in a uniform with faded insignia silently slipped out of an old timber house, clicking the back door quietly behind her. She held a large worn suitcase. Walking into a rundown shed she looked back to the house, checked the suitcase lock for the hundredth time, then placed it in a large wooden barrel.

She flicked invisible dust from her uniform, smoothed her unruly blonde hair, then moved with light footsteps across the paddock to the gate of the property. Once there she tapped a low-heeled shoe nervously as she looked back and forth, here and there.

The house was hidden from the road by dense grevilleas lacking the care of a gardener's hand. Only a thin curl of upward smoke, evidence of a dying fire, conveyed the presence of a dwelling.

The wooded section of their land, thick with eucalypts, undergrowth and leaf litter appeared foreboding in the shroud of the receding night. Gradually, the fog thinned slowly to the base of the trees, lifted by a moaning wind, shredded like worn fabric.

A lone car passed, fog lights piercing the haze.

The woman moved quickly to gain concealment behind the grevilleas but she'd been seen—a hand movement from the car, an odd salute, an unknown driver. She responded with a slight rise of her hand. The car was not familiar. And those fog lights, unusual for the small community.

The woman checked her watch. The taxi would be here soon. She unlatched the gate, crept into the shadow of the thickest gum tree.

A light came on in the house. The woman flinched, stepped onto the gravelled verge.

A rustling of grevilleas made her look back.

Away

With chipped black nails Bridget tore at the grey, stained bandage on her wrist as footsteps down the narrow hallway grew louder. *Go away. Go away.* The heavy oak drawers she had hastily shoved against her bedroom door would only slow his progress a little if he really wanted to come in; if he had some complaint, a breaking of one of his ever-changing rules. Or just a filthy temper. She strained, listening for the slap slap of his leather belt; the thick, studded one he most often used to punish her. She couldn't hear the sound.

She clutched a small paring knife, wishing she had the courage to use it on him, instead of cutting herself to relieve the ache that was stronger than the sting of the blade.

The bandage loosened and coiled to the dull carpet that had once been flecked with blue—those years ago before Mum left. Without her. Tears fell in silent hot splashes on her black T shirt. The footsteps slowed. Don't stop. Keep going. Go away.

Her older brother, Byron, was hardly ever there to offer

3

begrudging protection. He came home for a few days sometimes, even though he'd moved out to an upmarket apartment with his mates and a superior class of weed.

She heard the toilet flush. Silence, then shuffled staggering back to the kitchen.

She'd given Da his tea and a six pack of beer. Even cooked his favourite sausages and mash. She hadn't brought the salt and tomato sauce straight away—she didn't want to make him suspicious by trying too hard.

The sound of cutlery clinking on the plate resumed, then stopped. He'd finished his meal. She heard the hiss from one, two, three and then four cans of beer. She was safe now. Throwing the knife across the room she began to rock back and forth, sobbing.

Minutes passed, then she heard the crash of dinner plates into the sink and Da's shuffling to his room. Reaching into a cavity at the back of her bedhead Bridget removed a dented biscuit tin with her name BRIDGET GALLOWAY scratched across *Shortbread Creams.*

She trimmed a kerosene lamp to a soft low glow, enough to light her way back to her room later, inched the timber window upwards, threw her backpack to the ground and slipped out into the darkness.

The cemetery was beautiful at night.

Worn and broken edges that jarred the eye in daylight couldn't be seen. Fractured edges of porcelain flowers shone, their faded hues and stained centres muted by the indigo night.

Bridget sat beside the grave of the infant Thompson twins, gliding light fingers along the marbled silk of the headstone. The white stone angels were pristine, glinting softly with early morning dew in the surrendering light of the moon.

She took out the battered tin she'd brought, found a new sheet of thick art paper, sorted through her charcoals and began. With quick deft strokes, she sketched an outline of the angels, stopping now and then to smudge soft shadows with her fingers. Shading: light, dark, soft, harsh.

The cemetery was the most private place on earth. Her only refuge. Away from the cramped grime of the house where Da was absolute master, with his bitter spitting words, quick fists and whisky-sour breath.

It was Bridget's sixteenth birthday.

Ten years to the day since her mother had left. Bridget still couldn't understand why her mother ran off with a sales rep. Not on the eve of her daughter's sixth birthday. Bridget had seen the cake decorations at the back of the pantry. Her prying fingers had found a handmade butterfly card in the craft cupboard, sketched with Mum's pastels.

She'd pretended not to know.

Her mother's eyes had twinkled with mischief when she'd tucked Bridget in the night before, wrapping the small girl in her own guilty possession—a cashmere shawl, the palest blue Bridget had ever seen. Winter's icy breath had seeped through the valley. There were few all-night fires anymore.

As her mother bent down to kiss her, Bridget saw split skin on her mother's forehead as her hair fell forward. Bridget touched the wound. 'Silly me,' said her mother, collecting the eggs from the henhouse in the dark again. 'I'm such a tripper.' Her mother did a little dance.

Then, just before dawn, her mother's kiss, and the soft promise—'everything changes today. You'll see…'

In the morning Bridget was cold and shivering. Her mother's shawl was gone. That night she didn't come home from her job at the dry cleaners.

Ten long years later, Bridget still walked past the dry cleaner's where her mother once worked, black hood pulled down over her eyes, lank black hair escaping the hood. As if she might see her mother working the till, serving customers with her bright smile and swinging blonde hair.

The Thompson twins had only lived two years. Not long enough to know the pain of this world, too young to hear angry, raging words, to see thundering fists.

Bridget touched an angel wing, exploring its curved perfection.

'I never thought I'd spend my sixteen birthday here, Mum. Stupid really. You're not even here. Sometimes I think it would easier if you were. Maybe that's why I'm here. I have no place for you. I still can't believe you left. Not on my sixth birthday. Not after saying "this will be a special birthday, you'll see". You went off to work, but you didn't come home. Da said you ran off with a chemical rep. When I told him you'd never do that he slapped my face, hard.' Bridget wiped her eyes with a sleeve.

'That's when it began.'

The parents of the Thompson twins had somewhere to

come and remember. But Bridget had no place, no place other than here in the cemetery among lost souls that belonged to other grieving hearts.

The factory whistle blew. 5:00 am.

Da would be waking soon. Bridget packed the charcoals carefully in the tin and stood, her long thin coat swirling like a dark shroud. She slipped into the scrub, another shifting shadow in the night.

She walked slowly, touching the chilled branches of the low eucalypts with reluctant fingertips, avoiding potted cracks in the bush path, carved by recent storms. She knew every shadow, the sheds, the narrow-laned paths, the looming curved mass of the mechanical gravedigger with its prehistoric head.

On the tarred road home Bridget found the fence line and trailed her fingertips along its tense strength, avoiding the barbs.

A horse whinnied softly, pranced to the fence and thrust a wet nose through the wire strands.

'Hello, Jessie. Waiting for me as usual. What have I got for you?' Bridget reached into a pocket and produced a half-eaten apple. 'Sorry girl, all I've got.'

The animal accepted the treat and bunted Bridget's shoulder.

Bridget stopped at the fence boundary to the Galloway property.

Something hard and cold formed around her. She was leaving herself behind, Leaving to become the shadow girl the kids at school avoided, the one with cheap clothes, old books and scuffed shoes, as unfashionable as they were ancient. She hesitated before parting the barbed wires. Once through them, she'd be nothing again.

Dead grass crackled underfoot as she moved across the yard, shoulders curved into the day. There was no vegetation on this part of the property. Bare and denuded from the days when Da ripped and tore every living thing from the ground. He'd been going to plant macadamias and olive trees. Back in the days before their mother left.

The house was quiet. Da must still be asleep. For how long, she never knew. If luck was with her, he'd sleep till noon. He was snoring loudly.

It was hours before school time. Bridget opened the top drawer of her desk, took out a slender cardboard box and went through the cards that her mother had sent since she left. Some were cards and some were brief letters. All in a flowing script with hearts throughout.

Somewhere out there. A world away from her daughter.

Bridget touched the cards, wondering if her brother Byron had received the same letters. He refused to talk about their mother, just like Da. The air that hung around Da was thick with menace at the sound of any reference to her.

It was confusing. The cards and small trinkets that came with the letters from her mother were carefully placed in Bridget's desk drawer. All was well as long as she didn't say anything. She'd heard the kids at school tell their divorce stories of parental wars, fights over contact, phone calls. It must have been a big deal for her mother to get cards past Da.

She hadn't received anything for her sixteen birthday, or the year before. That stung more than she cared to admit.

Something had gone wrong and there was no one to ask, no uncles, no aunts, no grandparents. Was Mum an orphan? Or was Da just as efficient at cutting off family as he was friends?

Mistakes

Bridget's **second** mistake had been to criticise Chris Green's esteemed novel *The Fault in Our Stars*. It went down about as well as Darwin's first airing of *The Origin of the Species*. It wasn't as if it had even been in English class, it was History with the much pitied Mr Neville Mangret, their gay teacher with no dress sense who was loved as much as he was pitied.

'It's a sanitised romanticising of death and teenage love where the adults in the book are all insipid characters that play off and pander to the ill-fated teens who, ALTHOUGH DYING, (she shouted this bit), fly alone to Amsterdam, stay in a 5 star hotel where they...' at this point Bridget registered the shocked face of Mr Mangret and her gaping classmates. She stalled, frozen in embarrassment. Bridget never spoke in class, and even to her classmates out of class. The less they knew of her, and she of them, the better.

Bridget's **first** mistake had been to head off to school on a day when her father had been roaring drunk on his 3am journey to the toilet the night before, and had thrown her 8-week-old kitten across the room, ending its life in a hideous shattering of limbs and fur.

Bridget had raged on the toilet door until her knuckles bled but Da had swiftly shoved her aside with such rage and speed that she had fallen, reaching and grasping the kitten's mute body as she fell.

After a fart and a thorough crotch scratching, Da had shuffled off to his room muttering, immune to Bridget's screams and cursing him as 'a monster, a hideous shell of a man, a horror show of a human being'. It was the first time she'd let loose the words that caused her head to throb with hatred at the kitchen sink when he complained about the food, her slowness in cleaning up, her general stupidity.

All the while, and every time he spat those words, a voice thundered and roared inside her head, that he was wrong, this man who never saw her distinction with her schoolwork, never spoke to a single teacher of her achievements and never laid eyes on a single stroke of art she'd produced at school. Those things were locked at the school or in her mind as she chanted through house chores, 'I am more, I will be more'.

Bridget tended the body of the kitten, cotton-woolled in a shoe box. Her angry steps crunched on the icy path that had once been the route to her mother's tomato patch. There she buried her pet.

Inside the house she had paced with a rage she'd never experienced before. Picking up a large kitchen knife she padded into her father's room where his sterterous snoring seemed as defiant and belligerent as his daytime ravings.

Even in sleep his fists were clenched, skin pale and wrinkled. A slant of moonlight on his faced showed a pointed chin, weak jaw, even whiskers. Fine red veins flushed his cheeks and thin crooked nose.

She held the knife at his throat, just below his hairy ear, between the sinews of his throat. Calm settled through her body.

How close she had been to ending her torment. How near demise he came, the monster who used his belt and his fists on her thin body.

Da had shuddered, snorted, sat up. He stared, not seeing, not knowing, then fell back, turned onto his stomach and resumed snoring.

His eyes, so devoid of anything human were more terrifying in the semi-gloom than his bloodshot daytime tirades.

Bridget had grabbed for the knife as it slipped. It cut her palm with a satisfying pain that brought her back to reality. She padded to her room where she sat staring at the frosted window pane until the dawning sun softened the ice, sending it downwards in faint jerking rivulets, leaving a clear view of the eucalypt scrubland.

In the morning, even without sleep, school had seemed a better option than a day in the house.

How wrong she'd been, she thought as she escaped red-faced into the maze of school hallways.

Mr Mangret hurried down the corridor after her, his moccasins a dull, sliding thud thud on the Lino. However, before his quick steps reached Bridget, she was intercepted by the temporary Welfare Teacher, bloody old-fashioned Mrs Prudence Wainwright whose fulsome bosom kept her perpetually leaning forward when she walked, pigeon-toed in hard heeled shoes.

'I heard all that kerfuffle, Miss Galloway,' said Mrs Wainwright, gesturing towards the counselling room.

Ushered into the tiny, book-lined office, Bridget held her backpack like a shield and sank into a chair while Mrs Wainwright clattered the blinds shut, slapped her hands back and forth on the sill as if to remove a decade's dust. The room smelled stale, in that unused way, perhaps because the coat rack was overflowing with teacher's coats, left to dry or perhaps forgotten by teachers seeking a hasty escape as she did then.

'Well, now. Well, now.' Mrs Wainwright lowered herself into the chair behind the desk, unlike the regular counsellor who favoured almost knee to knee contact and penetrating gazes.

Bridget stared at the dull carpet, her usual ploy to deflect attention and expedite matters. Anyway, today she didn't care about classroom rules, superior teachers or punishments.

'Now, I know that I'm casual here and don't know you as well as the other teachers, dear.'

Bridget coughed. Hardly any of the teachers acknowledged her existence. Apart from Mr Mangret, the Saint of Lost Causes. She could see him pacing through the gap in the door.

Mrs Wainwright, smoothed her high bun and continued. 'I know it's very popular, and rebellious for you young people to have this whole freedom of speech thing, but your behaviour in class was unacceptable. This interrupting loudly, then storming out of class. You caused quite a stir, an uproar certainly. Oh the students applauded, sure! But honestly?'

Bridget raised her eyes briefly, round with shock. Applause! Oh no!

'Insurgence really, anarchy, whistling, standing on desks, feet stomping—terrible!'

Bridget gasped. Had all that happened? It was hard to understand the woman. She spoke like someone's great-grandmother or a character from a television show set a few decades ago. And she rattled the words out so quickly. Bridget let the words wash over her. She pretended she was lying under one of the upturned boats on the pebbly shore at Noarlunga, the boat where the breeze still crept underneath or through a crack that allowed enough sunlight to read without the world knowing where she was…

'Have you cut your hand, child?'

'Huh.' Bridget jumped. 'Er.' Blood was seeping onto her uniform. A hastily applied Elastoplast had failed. Either that or the wound had reopened. 'Shit,' she said, snatching a handful of tissues and gripping them tightly.

'Are you alright, m'dear?' Mrs Wainwright attempted to stand but was foiled in this by her girth and the desk.

Bridget's head swirled. Hot tears gathered in her eyes but she held them back with the same tenacity that she guarded her words. Lips pursed, she sat in silence. At least her thoughts were her own. No, I'm not alright. My father murdered my kitten, my only true friend on earth and I stood over him for a full half-hour with a knife millimetres from his carotid artery but I chickened out and I wish I hadn't.

Finally she spoke. 'Yes, Mrs Wainwright, but I'd better see the nurse.' She leapt to her feet, scraped the chair backwards and ran out the door, fully aware that Mrs Wainwright had no chance of successful pursuit.

Friendship

'What do you two want?' Bridget scowled and adjusted her tatty blue backpack.

'Sheesh, chill will ya. We just wanna chat. You know, con—ver—sa—tion.' Jenna sat beside Ebony on the stone wall at the far corner of the school.

'Yeah, you expect me to believe that. You're part of the cool kids and you're not fooling me.'

This statement from Bridget set Jenna off. 'Osh b'gosh, what a load of manure. Cool kids? Us? What a laugh. As if you'd know anyway. You're always loping off to the art room.'

Bridget turned to Ebony. 'What's she on? Why does she talk like that?'

'Her mother's an actor. She has loads of different gibberish. She waffles in Shakespearean sometimes. Bloody annoying.'

'At least she has a mother.'

'Ha,' said Jenna, 'one who'd rather be on the other side of the world. "I'm just not cut out for motherhood, you do understand Jenna daaarrrling".'

'Shit, that's awful. What about you, genius?' Bridget glared at Ebony.

'Mine's dead. And it's no bonus to social standing at school to ... get good grades, Bridget.'

'Sorry, didn't know your mum ... was, anyway, sorry.'

Ebony moved to make a place for Bridget to sit between them. Bridget sat warily on the edge of the stone wall.

'No one, like, talks to me. Don't see why you two are being all friendly. Anyway, aren't you s'posed to be at school not sitting out here?'

'Nah, yeh,' said Jenna.

'Yeh, nah,' said Ebony, giggling.

Their attitude was infectious.

Bridget found herself grinning.

'No one talks to us either. We're both kinda new, and not being locals, well no one bothers,' Ebony said, pulling her long black hair tighter in her scrunchie.

'But your parents are important people around here.'

'Ha,' said Jenna, 'you try making friends when your father is a private detective. It's as bad as having a cop for a dad. And if you ask kids home they like expect food of some kind and my dad is useless in the kitchen. He forgets to buy snacks even.'

'And my dad runs the polyclinic, so he's onto all the medical and personal stuff, town secrets: so no one wants to hang with someone like me. You think you're the only one, but you're not. Honestly.'

'Yeah well, you don't know everything. I can't take friends to my place. My dad's a looney. You'd run like hell.'

'No we wouldn't,' said Jenna, standing and swishing her blonde ponytail assertively. 'Prove it.'

'All right. Don't blame me if it all goes to hell.' Bridget shrugged. This would sort them out. She had everyone waving to her at school since she'd spoken out and had the class rebelling. She didn't need fake friends, just interested for a day or week. She was better alone.

That's how the three girls came to be standing among the thick grevilleas at the front of the Galloway property. If all three were having doubts about the idea, no one said anything.

'Oh well,' said Jenna, stepping out from the shrubs, 'lead on McDuff!'

At the back of the house they found Mr Tom Galloway wearing his best shirt and conducting a smooth normal conversation with a woman in riding boots and a pale blue checked flannel shirt. They were sitting at a wrought iron table with papers in front of them and coffee cups beside the papers.

'Get us a refill will ya, Bridget lovey,' said Mr Galloway. 'And one fer yer nice friends too.'

'Fuck me,' said Bridget under her breath as she turned to go inside the house.

Ebony giggled, then hiccupped.

'Spoon of sugar will cure that, girlie,' said the woman with Galloway.

Everything was in place. The kitchen bore no sign of the lunacy Bridget had claimed.

Ebony stared.

Bridget wondered if the horsey woman had cleaned up

after Da's breakfast. She opened a green laminate door that was peeling at the edges and retrieved several mismatched coffee mugs.

'I keep the place up,' said Bridget, deflated.

'We don't want coffee,' said Jenna. 'Got Cola or something?'

Bridget shrugged and checked the fridge. She found three cans of Cola. 'Haven't got low sugar. Byron gets these.'

'Who cares, that'll do,' said Ebony.

'Your dad's a hard core drinker,' said Jenna. She jumped backwards effortlessly to sit on the kitchen bench, pulled back the teapot embroidered curtains to peer out of the window.

'What!' Bridget stopped putting coffee into mugs. 'How can you tell?' Jenna hadn't seen the beer in the fridge, or the spirits cupboard.

'Yeah, how can you tell, Jenna?' Ebony asked, popping the cola.

'Red veins on his cheeks, tremble with the cup. Bloodshot eyes. Hardly ever takes a break from the stuff, does he.'

'No,' said Bridget, voice low, fighting tears to realise that someone saw. 'Dunno how you worked that out.'

'And that noise we heard as we stomped around the yard before he saw us—that was beer cans hitting the bin. How am I doing, Bridget?'

Bridget nodded.

'Who's the horsey woman?' asked Jenna. 'Drinking buddy?'

'Nah. That's Carol. She agists the north paddock for her horse. Pays Da cash or does errands in return, gets groceries and stuff. Da reckons she "does his accounts" too, he's on a Vet's pension.'

'He's a Veteran?' Ebony asked.

'Yeah, never went to Vietnam though. Supposed to be deaf from cannon fire in practice, but he hears just fine if you ask me. And he's claimed PTSD. Doesn't hang out with the other Vets. I can understand why. Nothing in common. He was never there.'

By the time Bridget carried two coffees out to the table, the woman had gone. Da quickly folded the papers into a box. 'Took yer long enough, girl,' he said, cuffing Bridget on the shoulder and sending one of the coffee mugs onto the ground where it broke noisily. 'Jesus girl. I'll get yer for that. Clumsy bitch.'

Bridget shook and bent to pick up the pieces.

'Just get me a beer, will ya. If yer can manage that small job. Never seen a more useless female in all my life, cept for y'mother.'

Jenna and Ebony came out the back door. Bridget's father looked shocked.

'Who are you lot? Sneaking around a man's house? Git, go on, git.'

The girls took off, only stopping at the end of the long drive.

'I don't like leaving Bridget there,' said Ebony.

'This isn't just today, Eb. This is Bridget's life.'

'God almighty,' said Ebony. 'I had no idea, none at all. No wonder Bridget is like she is. We must do something.'

Yeah! what, little Miss Social Worker? It's not that simple.'

Ebony was quiet. Something, anything, had to be done.

'Why doesn't the brother do something? What's his name? Byron?' Ebony broke the silence.

'He only cares about getting high, Ebony.'

'How do you know all this, Jenna Bragg?'

Jenna tapped her nose. 'Sources, m'dear, sources.'

Ebony poked her tongue out and turned away.

Jenna muttered, 'Bastard, bastard, bastard' as they headed to their respective homes.

Bridget was mouthing similar words as she threw the shattered mug pieces in the bin and opened a beer for her father, then, keeping her distance, she placed it on the cast iron table, careful not to disturb the wobbly table leg Da had been meaning to fix for decades.

In her room, Bridget sobbed. She had gained and lost friends in one afternoon. Like always. She hadn't realised how much it meant to have friends and wished she could start over. Keep her home a permanent secret. Maybe then…

Ebony and Jenna were waiting for Bridget after class.

'Watcha doing?' asked Jenna.

'Going to the Palace of Broken Dreams and Crockery,' Bridget said, leaning her backpack against the stone wall where she'd met the girls the day before.

Ebony and Jenna leaned on each other and laughed.

'Hey,' said Ebony, 'we've now got the funny one.'

'What am I?' asked Jenna, letting her hair loose before returning it to a ponytail.

'The fiery one.' Ebony smiled. The kind of smile where the

smiler hopes they haven't offended.

'Fair enough,' said Jenna. 'I thought something a bit more forensic, like the sciencey one.'

'That's good too. And me?' asked Ebony.

'The hiccuppy one,' said Jenna.

Ebony reached for Jenna who took off at a run, but soon realised that taking on someone who breezed through track and field was best avoided.

Puffed and panting, Ebony sat on the wall. 'Don't ever chase that one,' she said to Bridget.

'Don't worry,' said Bridget, 'with those long legs she could run in the Melbourne Cup.'

By the time Jenna arrived back, Ebony and Bridget were laughing.

'Okay, Ebony, you're the smart one.'

Ebony, now rested, decided it was time that Bridget learned to ride a bike. Jenna offered hers. Both offered instructions.

It turned out that if Ebony was the smart one, that wasn't always the case. Bridget connected with the school wire fence with a shattering clank.

The polyclinic was deserted. Clinic nurse, Emma Harcourt had been in the process of locking the doors when Ebony, her stepdaughter waved manically at the side door.

The three girls traipsed in when Emma slipped the door aside. 'I see,' she said, 'three for the price of one is it? You'll owe me, you know.'

'We'll order pizza,' Jenna said, bowing deeply. 'And you can make those marvellous pancakes we all love.'

'Sit down, you lot. Honestly. Now, who's the patient?'

'Bridget.'

Emma rolled her eyes at the scant information.

There was a jagged cut under the girl's chin.

'Does she need stitches?' Ebony leaned forward in the chair, anxious eyes on Emma.

Bridget paled and began to tremble. Her eyes glazed.

Jenna, chilled about the whole process, was scouring through her backpack for some unknown purpose. 'She stacked my bike, but the bike's okay, so it's like no probs.'

'Let me have a look, honey.' Emma gestured to Bridget. 'You're Bridget Galloway aren't you?'

The girl's lank, black hair hung in stringy cords around her face.

'Take deep slow breaths, Bridget.' Emma grabbed a coat and put it around the girl's shoulders.

'Is she going to pass out?' Ebony put her arm around Bridget. 'She does that you know, pass out.'

'I don't want stitches. I don't want doctors.' Bridget's voice was shrill, afraid. She began to rock slightly, back and forth.

'You don't have to, honey.' Emma patted the girl on the knee and was pleased to see her relax. 'I see someone has given you first aid of a sort.' Emma eyed the bloody wad Bridget was holding against her chin.

'That was me. S'a handkerchief.' Ebony pulled on the hem of her school uniform. 'Thanks for seeing us, I mean Bridget.'

'You're lucky I heard the tapping on the back door. Only the staff come in that way and they don't knock.'

'We didn't want anyone to…' Bridget murmured.

'...know about it,' finished Ebony. 'But nosy Mrs Wainwright was in the carpark with another old duck. She saw us, and she's like the worst gossip ever even though she's supposed to be our temporary Welfare Counsellor. Is it true Bridgee doesn't have to see a doctor? She wouldn't go to the school nurse.'

'That stupid nurse would ring Da.' Bridget interjected.

'He's a filthy bastard,' said Jenna, scanning her phone. 'We escaped from school. I had to help Bridget through a gap in the fence.' Jenna sucked on sour lollies and handed them around.

'So I'm harbouring fugitives. Thanks for relieving the boredom girls.' Emma shook her head and chuckled. 'Honestly though, you don't have to see anyone, Bridget. No one will force treatment on you. That's not how we work. You always have a choice. Say yes, say no anytime. Why, you could just hold that old hankie on your chin as long as you liked. Of course, it might get stuck there.'

Bridget's eyes widened. 'Oh god, no. I'd rather you do it. Shut up, Ebony. I'm the patient. So, Da, my father doesn't need to know?'

'And you don't have to tell anyone? Even though we're minors?' Ebony asked. 'That's great! I sprained my ankle at school back in Sydney and our deputy head couldn't wait to get on the phone to Dad. I thought he was going to drive off the Harbour Bridge. He's so overprotective.'

Emma held out a hand. 'You're fifteen, sixteen, Bridget? You can get any kind of medical help you choose, clinic, doctor, counsellor. You have a right to confidentiality with treatment. Mind you, schools have different responsibilities, but we won't go there ... So, Ms Galloway, are you ready for me to take a look? I assume you didn't come here for the ambience or fascinating conversation.'

Emma worked quickly.

Ebony moved in closer, ready to protect her new friend. 'You alright Bridge? What are those things you're putting on ... Emma?'

'They're steri-strips, they'll hold the wound together instead of stitches.'

'That's a relief. I thought she'd need yards of stitches. Her head just split open. She bled like a geyser.'

'The scalp's like that.' Emma placed a small skin coloured dressing on the wound. 'What did she hit? Or should I say who?'

Bridget giggled. 'I...'

'She was trying to ride my bike,' offered Jenna, 'like I said. Stacked it. Hit the fence like a champion. She'll be right.'

'At school? Right?' Emma smiled. 'I guess you won't try that again Bridget, that's a shame. Bikes are great for kids your age.'

Bridget flushed. 'Oh no, I got really good in the end, well, *before* the end obviously. I'd love to ride around with Eb and Jenna.'

'Let me get you girls a drink. Tea? Coffee?'

'Oh we're right. We wouldn't want to bother you.' Ebony stood.

'Ah, you've heard of my coffee making ability. But I insist. I want Bridget to have something hot and sweet, for shock. So hot chocolates. We don't want her passing out on the way home.'

'Shit no. Oh, sorry.' Ebony flopped back in the chair.

Emma reached into a drawer, brought out an expensive chocolate bar and dropped a square into each cup.

Bridget leaned forward for the coffee and biscuits. 'Thank you, er, Emma, I thought Jenna was the motor mouth but Ebony has taken over this whole conversation so at least I can say thanks for myself.'

Ebony poked out her tongue for rather longer than necessary.

Outside in the carpark of the clinic, Bridget smiled and shuffled her feet. 'Thanks you two. You're good friends.'

'Woo hoo,' crowed Jenna, 'she used the F word, she called us friends. Friends. We're friends.'

'I didn't think … you'd want to bother with me, y'know, after meeting Da.' Bridget looked down.

'Well, there were consequences to that of course,' said Jenna grinning, causing Bridget to look up wide-eyed, 'we definitely don't want to be friends with your Da.'

Ebony giggled, then hiccupped.

'Hold your breath,' said Bridget, 'works for me.'

'Nah,' said Jenna, 'she's a hopeless case.'

Emma slumped in the chair after the girls left. She knew about the Galloways. There had been several occasions where the community nurses had to attend to Tom Galloway. His care notes mentioned various injuries from falls, but stopped short of calling the man what he was, a mean drunk.

She'd visited him herself. Not that Tom Galloway would remember her, or any of the other nurses who'd ministered to his breaks and cuts. He'd almost severed a finger once, manically chopping wood.

The Galloway house had been neat and clean for the most part. That was something. Now that she'd met Bridget, she realised the girl must be responsible for that. The old man had refused outside help with the house, even though he had a war veteran's Gold Card for premium service.

The son, Byron had been there then, steering between obligation and resentment. Wearing a suit, he'd looked out of place in the rundown house.

'Do I have to be here?' he'd asked, looking at his watch, a Tag Heuer. 'I've got to get back to work. My sister will be home from school soon. She'll see to the old dude.'

The musky aroma of marijuana had permeated the house, fighting with the odours of stale beer.

'That's what we're for, Byron,' she'd said, watching him bouncing on his heels.

'Great. Thanks Sister. Those mobile phones won't sell themselves.' He'd shot her a charming smile, a relieved afterthought.

Bridget had looked so afraid, and lost. It was entirely possible that the girl hadn't seen a doctor in years. She was too thin. Her black hair had seemed lifeless next to the other girls' glowing tresses.

She have to talk to Brady about getting Bridget a bike of her own. In a way that the girl's pride wasn't hurt. One of his youth programs should be able to manage that. She phoned him.

'Ah, for sure,' he said, 'she can have the bike I fell off when

I broke my leg. I didn't break the bike. Just scratched it heaps. I'll never get on the thing again.'

'But she needs a girl's bike Brady. There's a difference.'

'Hmm, ah...'

'Oh, for goodness sake, you fell off a girl's bike didn't you?'

'Maybe.'

Byron

'Did y'see that stupid cow?' laughed Benji. 'Jeez, you'd have to be pretty stupid to mess up going through a Maccas drive thru. What a moron!'

'Yeah,' said Byron. He hadn't seen, didn't want more chit-chat than necessary. He didn't want to be here, but he didn't have a choice.

Tonight was his date with Chloe. He smiled at the thought. She was a 10/10 for sure, pure perfection. Sweet and innocent, Chloe was ripe for the picking and Byron was going to be the one to pluck this delightful fruit. He'd been playing the good boyfriend for months now, longer than he'd spent on any other chick. But she would be worth it. He'd had to work hard for every kiss and caress. She was ready for this, and if she needed a little encouragement, well that's what Benji and his medicinal relaxation was all about. He couldn't wait any longer. It was time for this good girl to go bad. If he wanted hash for his big date tonight, he had to put up with Benji.

'You sure this gear's good?' Byron's eyes narrowed as he assessed Benji. 'It'd better be as good as what I usually get.' Byron didn't like changing suppliers, but he had no choice. Marty, his usual guy was 'out of the country'. Byron suspected he'd been arrested but he didn't want to know.

'It's the best, mate. Trust me,' said Benji.

Yeah right. Byron didn't like the look of this guy. His usual supplier wore a suit and tie; there was something about this new guy that didn't sit well. He was far too casual about the whole business. And he was grubby and unshaved. Missing his front teeth with the others a shade of black that probably meant they would follow. Didn't the guy have any basic hygiene? At least he'd learned that from his mother before she left. But this dude must've been raised by wolves. Byron didn't like a supplier who looked like he used way too much of the stuff himself.

'Don't play me, you little creep.' Byron snatched the plastic bag for a closer look. 'Lots of seed. Looks all right. It'd better be. I'll know where to come lookin'…'

'It's high grade, mate. I've got a reputation to keep. Been doin' this longer than that fancy pants Marty of yours. This will get you what you want from your ladee …' said Benji with a cocky smirk. 'And if it don't, I've got these little beauties …' Benji tapped the pocket of his flannel shirt. The sleeves had been torn off, revealing a dragon tattoo on his skinny arm.

Byron cringed, not wanting to know what Benji had in that pocket. The less he knew, the better. Probably Rohypnol, the date-rape drug. He recoiled from the thought.

'I don't need any gear to impress my women,' he said. 'Anyway, this girl's special. It's her first time. I just want her to chill out. In fact, I don't need this stuff at all. I've got control. I'm not an addict. I'm just a weekend good-time dude.'

'Yeah. They're all special. I've heard about you, golden boy. Whatever you say.' Benji laughed. It was a rasping sound that triggered a coughing fit.

Byron balled his hand into a fist. He made a mental note to ask around for another supplier. But today, he needed this low-life. 'We're going to have to work out something better than this—if there's a next time. I don't plan on driving around in this stinking piece of junk just to score,' he said.

'Don't get y'knickers in a twist. I'll look after ya. I told ya. I'm not at the bottom of the ladder if you know what I mean. You're very lucky. This is about me being able to trust you. I was prepared to give you a discount if you could help me out with storing some of the product ... but ...'

'Well, maybe I could help with that ... I mean, there's just me and the old man at the house, and he's drunk every day, all day.'

'Might be a possibility,' said Benji. 'There'd be a few grand in it for yer, along with the discount.' He smirked. The mention of Byron's boss had had the desired effect. Benji really needed a place, or more correctly, a stooge. Having a small stash for personal use was one thing with the cops, but the rapidly growing demand meant he was walking a fine line, and Byron might come in handy.

At the mention of Dave, his boss, Byron was impressed. He

had suspicions his boss Dave enjoyed the odd toke on the weekend. Come to think of it, he'd seen him with Benji at the nightclub. He strained to remember the circumstances.

'You've probably seen me at "Levi's". Bitchin' place that. I'm the Friday night DJ. Can't sneeze at that gig. What's your girl's name?'

Byron was silent.

'Jeez mate, just making conversation. Not askin' ya to donate a kidney. Sheesh! I'm older than you kid, you might be grateful for someone looking out for you someday. Well, good luck with ya date, mate,' laughed Benji, setting off another coughing seizure.

Byron was relieved when Benji dropped him back at the house. Frowning as he swung the gate open, he wondered why he bothered to even visit his mad drunk father and weird sister, much less stay there between flats. Money. Yeah. That was it. But he'd be making real money soon. His sales at the mobile phone store were going through the roof. His bonus at the end of the month would give him enough for an apartment overlooking the beach. Then he wouldn't have to make out in his car anymore, or pretend he lived at one of his mates' luxury units. Then he wouldn't have to consider Benji's offer.

As he went down the hall he noticed Bridget's door was shut and soft music was playing. What was the deal with her? He went straight to his room. There was no need to go to the lounge room where the old dude would be drunk on the couch watching telly.

At least the old man wasn't yelling at Bridget. The poor kid practically shrunk around their father, even when he was in a good mood, which wasn't often—only in that early happy 'had-a-few' stage, before he slumped into brooding silence. Then it was anyone's guess where he'd head next. Violent outbursts or passing out.

What would happen to Bridget when he left for good? He didn't want to think about it, so he pushed it to the back of his mind, remembering Chloe's sweet cherry kisses. She'd been driving him wild long enough. Tonight was the night. Throwing on a clean shirt over jean shorts, he flicked gel into his hair.

Smiling broadly, he knew he looked good. Thank goodness he didn't have too many of the old dude's genes. Although who'd know what the old lush looked like twenty years ago. Their mother was long gone. She was the lucky one. She'd run from this rat house before it pulled her down—gone with the first man who'd have her. That was their father's version anyway. And who was there to argue?

As he slipped quietly back down the hall he heard the lock click on Bridget's door. Jeez, he'd never work his sister out. She should be getting ready to go the beach, hanging out with friends, like every other normal teenager, not locking herself in her room at the slightest noise.

Almost

Leah Bond, ingénue genius fashion designer fresh out of an award winning stint at Sydney TAFE, with her own fashion line, stood in the centre of the white high-gloss kitchen of the upmarket home she shared (infrequently lately) with her much older husband, James Antoine, mystery man, entrepreneur and importer of expensive handbags. A man who spent more time in Thailand and their inner-city Sydney apartment. James Antoine employed a number of bodyguards that a reasonable person would be forgiven for mistaking as ex-cons. Even smart suits, supplied by James, did little to downplay this impression.

James Antoine had lately expressed serious concerns for his wife's mental health to anyone of their acquaintance, anyone who would listen to his narrative of Leah's apparent unravelling.

Leah was currently undertaking a strange occupation that would have added credence to her husband's claims, that is, if they hadn't known the real story, which is often not what anyone thinks it is. Leah crushed several flowers in her hands, rending and tearing them. Destroying their annoying, bloody cheerful little daisy faces. It felt good to be doing something, however small and impotent.

She placed their remains on the black marble bench and began to dice them, smaller and smaller, mesmerised by the rocking motion of the knife and the sharp metallic sounds of blade on stone. Her hands were green-stained and slimy, but still she pared, this way, that way, as if she were preparing basil for pesto. Something ordinary.

Life had been ordinary once.

Leah saw her reflection in the stainless steel range-hood. Fear haunted her eyes. Mascara had blended with her tears and made a grotesque path down her cheeks. A purple bruise was beginning to show on her neck. Her face belonged in a horror movie. Was she losing her mind? James seemed to think so.

She wiped her face with a linen tea towel. James hated that, she'd have to throw it out. She stared at it—smeared with black and green, indelible stains.

Her hands began to shake uncontrollably. She slid to the floor beside the huge metal bucket containing the rest of the daisies. She'd only destroyed a few, there were still dozens. Romance, she decided, began and ended with flowers. The profuse arrangements of courtship, then the showy garlands of apology. And of course, the guilt bouquet, the most extravagant of all. Life with James had jerked through many phases of excess, always excess.

Leah caressed a daisy, turning its face toward her. 'It's not your fault,' she said, 'you're only flowers.'

The phone rang. She jumped. She'd better answer it. It could be James, asking if she'd received the flowers. If she didn't get there in time there'd be more hell to pay.

'Hello,' she said, flinching at the rasp in her voice.

'Are you all right Leah? You haven't done anything stupid have you?' James' voice had an icy edge.

'I'm fine, honey. Just a tickle in my throat, dust, cleaning.'

'Are you sure? You haven't been yabbering on the phone to one of your friends, have you? Stephanie says there's still a mountain of work to be done for the show.'

'Tell my sister,' Leah said, 'that everything is on track.' She ground her teeth. 'Stephanie worries too much.

'She cares. She's your sister.'

Leah's hand cramped on the phone. *My sister, and your spy.* 'I'm putting you on speaker phone James. I ... have my hands full here.'

'You know I hate that Leah. Anyway, I haven't got much time. Did you get the flowers?'

'Yes. I got them.' *All six dozen of them.*

James was silent.

'They're lovely. Thanks, honey.'

'Well, I wanted ... to make it up to you.'

Leah froze. Not the apology, the contrition that looped back to recrimination, then blame.

'Leah? You there?'

'Yes.'

'I'm sorry babe, but I have to go overseas, urgent business.'

'How long?'

'Two weeks. I'm sorry to miss the show ... and

everything…'

Leah tried to concentrate. Two weeks, two weeks free of James. He was cajoling now. She mustn't seem pleased.

'But James, you promised.'

'I'll make it up to you. Bring you something wonderful from Thailand. Anyway, we can skype. Every day. It will be just as if I was there with you. Just don't do anything stupid, like before … okay honey bun?'

'I'm fine I said.'

Like before … before when James had gashed her wrist with the quick slice of a knife, called the ambulance and babbled on about her mental state while she bled like a pig, protesting his version of facts that was rejected out of hand by the ambos and emergency staff. However, because it was the first incident she hadn't been admitted to the Mental Health Unit. That wouldn't be the case next time.

After Leah put the phone down, a tap on the glass door startled her.

It was Dyan, from next door. She pointed to the lock on the sliding door and mouthed, 'Open it, now!'

'I was just dicing…' Leah said.

'Daisies?' Dyan folded her arms. 'Don't bullshit me, Leah. I work in a women's refuge.'

'Oh.'

'Yes, *oh*! James isn't here I take it? Ah, no, of course not. You wouldn't have let me in … and don't tell me, James doesn't even know that you and I are acquainted. I'm not on that teeny weeny list of "suitable friends". Dyan mimicked quotation marks with her hands. 'Will James, Lord and Master, be home anytime soon? I wouldn't want to rock the balance of the high-walled kingdom.' Dyan raised an eyebrow, her face stony, as if she would relish doing precisely that.

Leah stood silently in the centre of the kitchen.

Dyan leaned on the bench, eyes narrowed.

Leah gripped her hand and flinched in pain. 'Dyan... Fuck!'

'Show me.'

Leah lifted her arm and unwound the bandage. 'It's my wrist. Months old now, but I get...'

'Keloid, yes, I see. Let me dress it. You need the right cream for it.'

Leah paled. 'I know. I just...'

'Haven't gotten around to it. I do understand sweetie, more than you know. Things that are hidden always come into the light. What happened? Was it James? Can't have been you, you're useless with your left hand.'

Tears streamed down Leah's face. 'The ambos didn't believe me. James had them thinking I was off my rocker.'

'There's a word for that.'

'I know Dyan. Gaslighting.'

'Have you had enough, Leah?'

'What?'

'You know what I mean.'

Dyan sighed, then, when she spoke, there was a new gravity to her words as her eyes pinned Leah. 'I thought I'd let you know that Peter and I will be moving his mother into the granny flat at the back of our place. It will be a bit noisy and busy over at ours for a few days. Workmen, **removalists**...'

'Removalists?'

'Yes ... they're usually thrilled with a return load, the truck will be here first thing in the morning.'

'In the morning...?'

'...first thing.'

Leah dragged the suitcase to the luggage check-in area at Sydney airport. She was catching the 6.00 am flight to Perth. It was a far as she could go without leaving the country. She glanced at her ticket. For the next few hours, she was Dyan Wilson. Just as well it was a domestic flight with no passport or ID checks. She'd done the flight check-in online and with the Q bag tag attached to Dyan's suitcase, she didn't even need to worry the luggage check-in staff. The process was familiar enough, she'd often seen James off on overseas trips.

Leah fumbled with the heavy suitcase and tugged at the brunette wig. She'd have to stop doing that. She went through security with ease, feeling like a criminal. Glancing at her watch, she realised she had time to kill, two hours. The airport buzzed with early morning activity. Feeling exposed in the crowd, she stepped into a pharmacy and tried on sunglasses. Catching her reflection in the mirror, Leah saw that the wig failed to cover the dark bruising on her neck. She quickly selected a chiffon scarf, and paid the assistant with trembling hands. The woman frowned.

'I hate flying,' said Leah, 'I get so sick and...'

'Do you want me to ask the pharmacist for something that might help?'

'No thanks, I'll be fine.' She forced a smile. 'It's just flight nerves.' Leah found a Ladies Room. Delving into her purse she found the yellow Valium Dyan had given her. 'Don't take it too early', she'd said when she handed it to Leah. Now would have to do, there was no way she was going to try and pop a tablet into her mouth in the waiting area. The wig was not her style, but it covered her own two-tone hair that she was attempting to grow out. At least it was her original colour, taking her back to her younger self. Back when she was safe. Before wealth and corporate success. Before James.

Leah felt a pang of apprehension. Not long now. Soon she'd be on a plane to West Australia. Home free; away from James.

Even now, she expected a heavy hand on her shoulder. Willing herself to relax, she drew in a measured breath.

She entered the waiting area at gate 32, and instinctively sat in the farthest corner so she could observe, without being seen. She could see the huge 747 through the floor length glass windows. A new wave of fear hit her. Glancing at her watch, Leah realised she still had over an hour to kill. Her throat was tight with tension. She'd done everything she could think of to avoid being found out. She was flying economy, her ticket was in another name … and yet dread had a stranglehold. It was hard to swallow.

What else had Dyan said? Half a glass of wine wouldn't hurt to relax her. There'd be no wine service on the short flight, but Leah remembered an area in the corridor where a group offered wine tasting. She turned and looked back. Why not? If her throat became any tighter she wouldn't be able to speak.

'I'd like to try…' her voice came out in a rasp. 'Oh…'

'Spot of laryngitis?' said the young man, grinning.

'Stress.' Leah shrugged and turned her hands up in a gesture of defeat.

'I'll need to see your ID love. You look about 15, although that wig, honey … dreadful. Sorry. I'm much too blunt.'

'It's okay. I'll ditch it soon.' Leah rummaged in her purse. She hadn't been asked for her ID in years. All that makeup she usually wore must have made her look older.

'Okay honey,' said the server, flipping her ID over. 'So you need something medicinal? Something dry? Or sweet?'

Leah pointed to her choice and the man poured the wine into a plastic cup.

Several people arrived and made requests, giving Leah the opportunity to lean on the wall and sip the wine. One of the women stared at her. Leah looked for a rubbish bin, but finding none, she downed the rest of the wine and headed for the waiting area. Flipping open a magazine, she used it as a shield.

Her phone blipped. Not the new one she'd bought with Dyan. Her old phone. The sound made her flinch.

Carefully she looked through her purse, found the old phone—Stephanie. What could her sister want? Leah had taken care of all the business arrangements. Why had she trusted her sister? She'd called Leah a coward.

Leah switched the phone off. Could Stephanie yet manage to derail her escape?

Empty

Stephanie Bond clicked her nails in frustration and pressed the doorbell again. She'd been too angry to make any sense of Leah's distressed phone call. And her phone call to Leah a few minutes before hadn't been answered.

What was Leah doing? Had she finally lost it?

'I'm leaving,' Leah had said, in her early morning call.

'What do you mean—leaving?' Stephanie had been discussing plans for the upcoming fashion show. She'd waved her assistant aside.

'Don't ask questions, Stephanie. I'm leaving. Walking away, going. Leaving.'

'You can't be serious! This isn't like you…'

'Just listen for once in your life Stephanie. I'm only phoning you so that I'm not listed as a missing person and splashed all over the news with every reporter and cop in the country looking for me. I'm going. Don't ask.'

'But the fashion show? There'll be talk.'

'You'll handle it. But frankly I don't care if you cancel it.'

'Why, Leah? I don't understand,' said Stephanie. 'Are you ... ill ...? Surely you could stay for the show. It's tonight! What are a few days in the scheme of things?'

'There's nothing for you to do. Jill has everything in hand.'

A car horn tooted.

'I have to go,' said Leah.

'What am I supposed to say to James?' Stephanie asked.

Leah had wept like a child. 'Don't tell him anything, not yet. Please Stephanie. I've never asked you for anything. Just hold off telling him. For a week. It's important, you'll never know.'

This blunt statement only added to Stephanie's confusion.

'You're a coward, Leah,' she said.

Stephanie rapped on the door, then inserted the key James had given her. She'd sort this out. James had been right to worry about Leah's mental state. Leah had always been a bit nervous and shy, but now she'd really come unhinged. Perhaps it was just panic. Maybe she was inside the house now, shaking with nerves about the fashion show.

Her footsteps echoed as she entered the foyer. The house was cold. She walked through the rooms. She couldn't believe what she saw. The house was completely empty. Not a piece of furniture in sight.

Just a note on the kitchen bench in Leah's scrawl, 'James', and her wedding ring.

Stephanie was furious. She slammed the door behind her.

'Excuse me,' said a silky voice behind her. 'Do you have a right to enter these premises?'

Stephanie turned to see an elegantly dressed young woman,

who held a 'FOR SALE' sign. 'I trust you can see yourself off the property.' The woman was accompanied by a workman who took out his tools and began to dismantle the lock.

Pausing on the grassy verge, Stephanie felt cold with shock and anger. He punched James' number on her mobile.

He had a right to know.

Dr Seuss

Leah only relaxed when she sank into her seat on the plane. She was safe, for the time being. Sighing deeply, she checked her watch. In just a few hours she could blend into the throng in Perth, find a cheap hotel, and then begin the last part of her plan, choose a small town destination to hide out in, a place to disappear.

Tears pricked her eyes. She might as well be going into witness protection, leaving everything and everyone behind. Her attempts to confide in her sister, Stephanie, had fallen flat. Like all their friends, Stephanie thought James could do no wrong.

'Half a plan is better than none.' Leah fastened her seatbelt.

'Did you say something?' asked the businessman beside her.

'Oh dear, I was thinking aloud. I hate it when I do that.'

'Only true geniuses talk to themselves, you know.'

'And there was me, thinking it was the other way around.'

'Things are never the other way around.'

'Are you related to Dr Suess, by any chance?' she asked, slightly annoyed she'd broken her rule not to converse with anyone. But this man's eyes were more amused than provoking, and it wasn't a good idea to be too paranoid.

'I wish,' he said, laughing.

The engines roared into life. The airline staff began the usual emergency spiel. Leah took in slow breaths, held them then exhaled. She felt lightheaded.

The man opened a newspaper, deftly folding it. The plane thrust upwards. 'Oh crap!' she said, gripping the armrest with iron fingers.

'Ouch!' muttered the man beside her. 'When did you win your last arm-wrestling competition?'

Her cheeks flushed. 'I'm so sorry.' She relaxed her grip on his arm.

Leah felt oddly relaxed, even though she had only managed a few hours' sleep in the past few nights. Freedom and safety were in reach. She even peeked out of the window and found herself lost in the view. She'd chosen the window seat to limit interaction with her fellow passengers, but that didn't seem necessary. After their initial few words, the man beside her became engrossed in a crossword.

When the stewards came with the catering trolley, Leah ordered a cup of tea and a muffin, hoping it would quell her nausea.

When the man beside her handed her the insulated mug the scarf fell over her face and she felt a wave of dizziness.

'You could take it off.'

Leah jumped in alarm. 'Excuse me?'

'I meant the scarf.'

Leah looked at the man. His face was hazy. Seeing only mild amusement, she decided he was harmless. She liked harmless men. This one had unruly chestnut hair. Not a control freak then. In her experience control freaks did not have unruly hair that curled over their collars. She leaned in a little closer, so that his face came back into focus. She accepted the tea and returned to the window.

'Here's your muffin,' said the man.

'Oh, thank you,' she said, leaning in to accept the box.

The plane shuddered with turbulence. Leah's head hit the man's chest. As she pulled back, the scarf became stuck on the pink ribbon badge on his suit. Leah straightened and grabbed at her wig.

The man smiled as he looked at the scarf, which now hung loosely around her neck with his badge attached.

'Oh dear,' she said, trying to focus, 'you're fuzzy.'

'You're messy,' he replied. 'But in a good way.'

'No, no.' Leah wished the cabin would stop spinning. 'I'm never messy. It's not allowed. *James says* it's unprofessional, James requires perfection—anything less is not acceptable.' She waggled her finger.

The man smiled. Perhaps he didn't aspire to perfection. 'Nothing wrong with messy,' he said.

'D'you think so?' Leaning in conspiratorially, Leah whispered, 'I'm never going to be perfect again.'

'Glad to hear it. I'd happily join as founding member of that club.'

'You're welcome. I'll make you CEO.'

'I accept.'

'You haven't heard the job description.'

'Oh, I think 'imperfect' covers it nicely. I'm sure I can manage that lofty standard.'

'I feel funny.'

'You might be a little tipsy?'

'Never … I'm just … not myself, you know.'

'Really, who are you?'

'Well, I am myself, obviously. But I'm not the self I was when I got on this thing.'

'Are you old enough to be tipsy?'

'Yes,' she beckoned him closer and whispered, 'I'm 19. Back to front, that's 91. I feel 91.'

'Things are never back to front,' he said.

'I like you, Dr Suess.'

The plane shuddered and jerked. Dark clouds replaced the sunny view. Leah's eyes filled with fear. The scarf tugged at her neck. She pulled it off. The man beside her took her cup and stowed it. 'Are you all right?'

'Yes, no. I hate flying, I never do it. I'd rather crawl. I'm so scared.' Her voice broke. She shivered.

'Why didn't you?' he asked.

'Why didn't I what?'

'Crawl.'

'You're funny, Dr Seuss.'

'Am I? No one else thinks so.' The man gestured for a steward. He asked for a blanket and placed it around Leah. The turbulence juddered the plane as lightning flashed. 'Here, grab my arm.'

'We'll die together, Dr Seuss. S'been nice knowing you.'

The Captain's calm voice came clearly over the loudspeaker. 'Ladies and gentlemen, I have to advise you that due to storm activity we have been redirected to Tullamarine Airport in Melbourne. Qantas wishes to apologise for any inconvenience, but the safety of our passengers is paramount. When you arrive in Melbourne, you will be given assistance with transport and accommodation if necessary. We would like to reassure you that every attempt will be made to ensure your comfort during the stopover. We anticipate that it will be no longer than 24 hours before flights resume. We will begin the descent shortly and ask that you return to your seats, fasten your seatbelts and cooperate with staff. Thank you for your patience.'

When the plane landed Leah struggled with her carry-on case. The man opened the overhead storage and efficiently plucked it out. Deftly, he steered both of their cases downstairs. Sensing her embarrassment, he passed her case over with a gentle, 'Okay?'

'Yes. Thank you. For everything. Oh, here...' She tried to unpin the pink badge from her scarf.

'Don't worry, you keep it.' With a casual nod of his head, he was lost in the crowd.

In spite of the promise of organisation, the airport was chaotic. Backpackers, obviously used to unpredictable lives, didn't bother to queue, but curled up on sofas. Parents calmed children. Airport staff dealt with customers. Some complained loudly and others sighed with resignation. There were two queues, one for the airport hotel, and one for a hotel in the city. The queue for the airport hotel was horrendously long, so Leah headed for the city hotel queue.

She didn't want to sit around in a crowded airport. Suddenly using Dyan's name seemed a mistake. Things were becoming more complicated. She hadn't come far at all. She'd often thought of leaving James, but the truth was that there was nowhere that felt safe. Walking out of a door didn't mean walking into safety.

When she arrived at the queue she was told that the hotel was booked out.

'That'd be right,' said a man behind her. 'We should've stayed in Noarlunga, Bren. This holiday lark has been nothing but a pain. Storms in Brisbane, then the nonstop flight to Adelaide buggered up. We're cursed.'

'Really, John,' said the woman with him, 'let's sit down and wait. I'm starving. Let's have a sandwich—you're making me nervous with your twitching.'

'There's no use, mate. The hotel is booked out,' said John to a man who was approaching the queue.

It was Leah's flight companion. The man she'd called Dr Seuss. Sober now, she turned her back. 'Ah, the vagaries of travel,' he said, smiling. 'You two look lost.'

He walked around the couple and noticed Leah, 'Oh hello, we meet again. Bad luck.'

'Is it? Oh … sorry,' said Leah.

'I didn't mean meeting, I meant the whole flight debacle.'

'It's now an accommodation debacle,' said John.

'He needs a sandwich,' said Brenda.

Adam laughed and loosened his tie. 'I'm Adam Price. I'm a solicitor from Glenelg, near Adelaide. I tell you what, I know a nice little hotel in the city. If I can get some rooms do you want me to book you in? We can share a taxi.'

'Wonderful,' said John, shaking his hand. 'John and Brenda Burnside.'

The three turned to Leah. 'Oh, me? Oh, yes please.'

'What a relief,' said Brenda.

'Do they have sandwiches?' asked John. 'Ouch, don't slap me, Brenda. It was your idea.'

Brenda walked beside Leah. 'You know that man, Adam?'

'We were seated next to each other on the plane,' said Leah.

Bren smiled. 'Oh, how convenient. We're practically all old friends then. A crisis will do that, don't you find? One dispenses with the formalities.'

'Bren, you've never been on speaking terms with any formalities,' said John, a teasing smile on his face.

'This is a gorgeous place, Adam,' said Brenda. 'What a gem.'

'Isn't it. My company uses it all the time.'

Leah stood back from the others when they checked in. Something wasn't right. Her new phone had pinged several times. Dyan had been trying to call her. She'd have to wait until she had a room. But now she had a new problem. Would they accept cash? She had decided to pay everything with cash so her location couldn't be traced. She'd opened a new bank account, transferring all her money there.

The receptionist called her.

'Can I pay with cash?' Leah asked, reaching into her purse for a roll of notes.

'I'm sorry, we don't take cash,' said the woman. 'Do you have a credit card?'

'Um.' Leah swallowed hard. 'I ... it's a new account.'

'Your name, Miss?'

'I'm ... it's.' Leah fumbled in her purse.

'You're not yourself?' Adam Price, aka Dr Seuss, appeared beside her. 'Not the self that got on the plane?'

'Something like that,' she said, suddenly weary.

Adam sighed and murmured softly. 'I'm going to regret this in the morning, but here goes.' He leaned towards the receptionist. 'This is Mrs Adam Price, put the bill on my tab.'

Leah sucked in air.

'Adjoining rooms, if you can stretch to that,' he said, glancing at Leah. 'My wife needs a great deal of rest.'

'Thank you,' she whispered. 'I'll pay you. Honestly.'

'You can explain later,' he said, placing a light hand under her arm and leading her towards the lift. 'On the other hand, maybe I don't want to know.' He turned to John and Brenda. 'See you two for dinner? It's on me tonight.'

Leah regretted not giving her name. She'd gone back to her maiden name. Leah Bond. It wasn't possible to change to any old name in the age of cyber-technology. As it was she'd had to fork out $200 to legally go back to her maiden name.

After the meal, Adam spied a chess board set up in the corner. 'Do you play?' he asked John.

'Yes, but I have to warn you, I'm a mean player.'

'Oh, you're on, mate!' Adam laughed.

John was a thoughtful player. Planning each move, then hesitating. There was a stoop to the older man's shoulders. Adam put that down to his past as a trucker. He was enjoying the game. John was a genuinely nice guy, and Bren was a delight. The two women had obviously bonded too.

Adam turned from watching the two women to concentrate on the chess game. They'd talked freely over the meal. The woman's name was Leah Bond. For the first time since he'd met her she was relaxed and smiling. He noticed she declined wine at dinner. As she chatted to Bren, she seemed serene. But if he was a betting man, he'd lay odds that she was going through some kind of crisis.

He noticed her twisting her engagement ring. That was some rock. Whoever Leah Bond was, she was seriously rich. Or her fiancé was. Looking down at his own ring finger, he wondered why he was still wearing his wedding ring. Caroline had died two years ago of breast cancer. And now the pink badge he usually wore, was on the scarf of another woman. It felt wrong. He'd bought that badge when they'd first found out. Six months to live. Caroline's iron will had eked that time into eighteen months. A time of happiness, and hell.

Bren watched John walk to the table. Smiling, she said to Leah. 'It's so good to see him relaxed.'

'I take it that doesn't happen often?'

'No. John has Post Traumatic Stress Disorder. It's slow progress, but he's improving. Anyway, where are you from, Leah?'

'Sydney, but I'm relocating. Not sure where yet ... I'm checking a few places out.'

'You were flying to Adelaide. Is that on your list? It's a wonderful city. We love it. Sorry, I sound like an estate agent, which I am incidentally, property management.'

'Oh. Adelaide is just supposed to be a stopover on the way to Perth.'

'You don't sound sure.'

'I'm not sure of anything right now. Sorry, it's a long story.' Leah looked away. 'I think I might holiday somewhere for a while...'

'You'll work it out. You look like a capable young woman to me, Leah Bond.'

Leah hoped that revealing her real name wouldn't come back to bite her. She simply couldn't lie to these lovely people. She would explain somehow if she got the chance.

'Tell me about the town where you live, Bren.'

'Noarlunga?'

'Yes. I overheard you mention it.' Leah looked out of the window. The hooded look had returned to her eyes. 'How is John this morning? Rested?'

'Yes, but he's had enough of air travel. He wants to go back by train. We'll look into getting on the Indian Pacific.'

'Oh that's marvellous, I've always loved train travel. I hate flying.'

'Leah, I hope you don't think this is presumptuous, but I have an idea. Please hear me out. You could come and stay with us. We have a separate granny flat at the back, you'd be quite private. Noarlunga is rather off the beaten track, it's south of Adelaide. It might give you a chance to have a breather, have that holiday time. It's as good a place as any...' Bren handed Leah her realtor's business card.

'I don't know ... but ... thanks.' Leah accepted the card. It could be a solution, a plan. She had an option, a place. It might not be much, but it was more than she'd had in a long time. 'I'll think about it, I promise.'

'Look at it this way,' chuckled Bren, 'you have an entire day to make up your mind.'

'That long!' Leah smiled.

The door in the large room was the only sign that Leah's room was connected to Adam's. In a hotel room, in another State, where no one knew her she was safe. After looking at the supper menu her stomach growled. Hot chocolate and croissants for two. Lightly tapping on the adjoining door, she waited for Adam's response. Thankfully he answered quickly because she regretted the decision as soon as she'd tapped on the door.

'Um, I'm thinking of ordering hot chocolates and croissants. It comes for two. I don't think I can...'

'Yes, love to. Why don't I order and you can wait in my room. There's a great movie on, George Clooney.'

'Oh Dr Suess. I can never resist The Clooney.'

'It's called Saggy Bottom Boys or something like that.' Adam drew a coffee table towards the couch.

Leah laughed. 'That sounds like a classic.'

When she moved into the room Adam was able to see her hair, short raffish and dyed blonde with dark roots well on the way to equalling the blonde. 'So that's what's under that, er ... interesting wig,' he said, 'your hair looks like one of those half dark, half white chocolate bars.'

'Right,' said Leah, settling onto the couch, 'that's backhanded compliment if ever I heard one.'

'I'm offended,' Adam said, 'I like chocolate.

The refreshments arrived. The movie stalled the need for conversation. They laughed together.

Leah's head began to droop. Part way through the film she jumped up and said, 'that was great. Loved it. I'd better get to bed for I fall asleep on your couch.

Adam smiled. Leah had been asleep for the good part of an hour, snoring softly as she rested on his shoulder.

Silently clicking the lock on her side, Leah slipped into the king-sized bed. She still hadn't received a message from Dyan, and yet she couldn't shake the feeling that something was amiss.

Leah awoke rejuvenated and starving. With the immediate stress gone, her appetite had returned. Who cares, she thought. There was no more need for meticulous calorie counting. It was James who was proud of her being a size 6.

Rummaging through her suitcase, she brought out the scarf. She hated to wear it again, but she wanted to cover the bruises. Then she found a sleeveless turtleneck black top. Perfect. She tucked the scarf back in the case.

She'd phoned Bren as soon as she was awake. In the end it hadn't taken her a whole day to make up her mind. She would travel to Adelaide on the Indian Pacific with Bren and John. And then on to Noarlunga. They would leave that evening. She was surprised how easy it had been to decide, it just seemed right. The trip would take two nights, so she'd asked Bren to book a sleeper for comfort.

While the men had played chess she had filled Bren in on her situation with James, and her fashion label. Bren had tapped her nose, flicked open her laptop and booked them as three Burnsides. Leah had handed Bren cash for the fare. She felt a kinship with the woman. Maybe the mystics were right, everyone came into your life for a reason. Anyway, she'd always wanted to travel by train, yet never had the time. Life had been too fast, too furious. The rail journey was a side-track she was going to enjoy fully.

The day stretched out before her. She could explore a new city, see new things. All without the shadow of James. The dark face of fear would be far away today.

Her stomach rumbled. Ignoring the lift she flew down the stairs.

Damn, thought Adam. There she was. He was strangely drawn to this frail woman and he didn't like it. His gut twisted. She reminded him of Caroline. He'd been shocked when he first saw her. Thin as a rail and wearing a scarf, she reminded him of the ravages of cancer. Chagrined, he remembered that he'd recoiled from her at first. She brought back the past with wrenching clarity. It seemed you couldn't outrun grief. It didn't gradually rise like a fog, but zoomed like a roller coaster, often catching you unawares.

Walking towards her table he noticed her plate. Wow. That was one hell of a breakfast, and she was devouring it as if she hadn't eaten for days. She wouldn't stay skinny at that rate. And that would be a good thing. He wanted to join her. She intrigued him. He hesitated, then she looked up at him and smiled. Oh what the hell, he'd be gone soon. She was joining Bren and John on the Indian Pacific and he had an evening flight to Adelaide. He'd never see her again. What was the harm in sharing breakfast? Or the morning for that matter. He'd always liked Melbourne. He knew Leah had never visited and experienced a moment of anticipation at the thought of sharing some of his favourite places.

John and Bren joined them and they chatted comfortably. After breakfast they set off on a stroll. John pleaded a headache and returned to the hotel with Bren, while Adam and Leah continued walking. Leah turned her back when passing any man, but she bent down freely to chat to children, smiling warmly at their mothers. She'd shown an initial flicker of panic when Bren and John parted company with them, but she seemed to deem him safe.

Adam wondered why he'd chosen to join her. Was it to solve the puzzle that was Leah? She was unnaturally thin and wore long sleeves she nervously tugged down. An addict perhaps? He saw the straight slash of a scar on the soft inner flesh of her wrist that seemed recent.

Later, when the sleeves of her light jacket slipped down he saw the discolouring of old bruising on her forearms. Oval bruises, like fingerprints, sent a chill through him. She flinched at the site of a well-dressed man with black hair, and moved imperceptibly closer to Adam. Then remembering herself, she stepped quickly away. They wandered among the structures of artwork that dotted the walkways near the Yarra River. Their conversation was casual and smooth.

Unaware of his scrutiny, Leah appeared comfortable in his

presence. However, in the early afternoon, her phone pinged. She became flustered. An urgent task back at the hotel?

The stocky dark-haired man approached. Leah put her head down and leaned into Adam's chest, her heart racing. Adam could feel her warmth through his shirt, her thundering heartbeat. He drew her closer, putting his back between Leah and the stranger.

When they arrived at the hotel, Leah immediately excused herself and went upstairs. A text message from Dyan read:

James' bodyguard has been skulking at the house. Stole our mail.
CHANGE YOUR PLANS.

Later Adam found an envelope marked 'Dr Seuss' passed under the adjoining door. It contained cash for the hotel and meals.

He went downstairs, but Leah was gone. When he tried to check if she'd taken the business card he left, the maid was cleaning the room. He didn't see her again, and was surprised by the pang of disappointment he felt.

Shack

The shivering gum trees at the cemetery's edge trembled with the first soft raindrops of a summer storm, falling onto the upturned face of a dark-clad girl. She grabbed a faded denim backpack and ran to an abandoned shack once used to house the coffined-bodies of the deceased, prepared for viewing and internment.

Thick brush concealed the old stone building. Several windows had long ago been shattered by vandals who'd then lost interest in the building and moved on. Nature had reclaimed what man forgot.

One window, broken decades before had been haphazardly boarded up by the girl, who'd also sealed the cracks with tile grout taken from her father's shed after he had chosen the medicinal value of alcohol over the fruits of labour. Few in the area could remember that time, or that other version of the girl's father—so long had he ranted and rampaged at his family and anyone foolish enough to set foot on his neglected acres.

The girl clicked the door of the shack shut and peeled back the hood of her sweatshirt. Flicking on a tiny flashlight, she checked a neat pile of twigs and branches by the fireplace, gathered earlier.

Inside the hut, the earth was swept clean. Nature had not intruded here, due to the girl's diligence.

With charcoal-stained fingers she built a Tee-pee from the sticks, over a tea light candle, pulled from the depths of a tattered jean's pocket. Careful placement, flash of a match, soft breath on the straw as a flame flickered, then grew tall as the ancient chimney draught drew the flame higher. Twigs hissed and lent orange fire to the dry crackling branches.

The girl unfolded a grey blanket sitting on the lintel, checked her phone for the time, then gathered the blanket around her, nose wrinkling at its dank odour, and waited. Waited for the storm that loomed and threatened in the pitch darkness.

The door flung open, slamming into the daub inner wall.

Covering her mouth quickly to smother a scream and give voice to her presence, the girl cowered.

The intruder pushed the door shut. A panting human form slid down the closed door to the floor. A wide-eyed woman, too terrified to be a threat, opened her mouth in surprise as her eyes adjusted to the flickering firelight. She saw the girl trembling in the corner below a long thin window where lightning slashed through the room transiently as it taunted the earth with its power.

They stared, each assessing the other. The girl sat forward, blue eyes intense, silently asserting her frail dominance over the hut. After all, it was her domain. She'd shared this sanctum with no other.

A penetrating glare of torchlight hunted back and forth, piercing the storm and the night with ferocious intent. Here, there. Swiftly, swiftly.

As the light flicked towards the intruder, the girl reached across the small room and hauled the woman down to the floor, then beckoned her across the room to hide from the invasion of the light.

'Who's that?' said the woman, her voice a rasp, 'a caretaker?'

The girl shook her head, keeping a hand on the woman's shoulder.

Footsteps crunched, heavy-booted.

The girl used the blanket to smother the fire, repressing a cough at the smoke, a sound that was mercifully covered by thunder and the storm's renewed veracity.

They heard a curse, a growl. A swing of light, then darkness.

The silence was pitted by sharp, whizzing rain.

The woman sneezed.

A giggle, quickly extinguished, escaped the girl.

Brown eyes met blue.

The girl stoked the fire. A bandage stained with blood-rust spiralled from her left hand and caught alight. Cursing softly, she put out the flame with her right hand.

'Oh, doesn't that…?' asked the woman.

'Hurt?' The girl shrugged. 'No more than … whatever.' Looking closer she saw an Elastoplast on the woman's right wrist.

'Doesn't that hurt?' she asked, wry-smiling.

'No more than whatever,' said the woman.

They placed their wounded hands side by side, the girl's left hand, the woman's right, uncharacteristically joined by the stormy night and its peril, by their silence and seclusion. Their need for safety.

They fell silence, watching the flame cast leaping shadows on the walls, both reluctant for more conversation, both reluctant to leave.

As the room grew warmer, the brown-eyed woman threw off her dark coat, revealing a soft pink shawl with an unusual pattern. The girl leaned forward, entranced by the shawl. She reached out her hand to gently touch its softness. 'My mother had one like this, same pattern, but pale blue.'

'It's an old thing,' said Leah.

'Sorry,' said Bridget, snatching her hand back as she gathered her phone and backpack.

Bridget Galloway and Leah Bond parted with only a nod. Strangers.

Fading

At the Harcourt house, Jenna and Ebony were arguing.

'How can you two argue after pancakes like that?' Bridget moaned. There was a sting to her tone. 'You've been at it all morning. "My mother isn't coming home for my birthday". "Dad won't let us go to the Druid Nails concert". "Jack won't let me work in his office". Blah, blah, blah.'

'What's got into you, Bridget?' asked Jenna.

A plate clattered into the sink. Ebony and Jenna turned towards Bridget who was rinsing dishes.

Jenna moved towards Bridget. 'You okay Bridge?'

'Yeah. 'Course.'

'Your hands are trembling.'

'Whatever,' said Bridget. The word stabbed, jarring the two girls.

Bridget pulled a lank strand of hair behind her ear. She flushed. 'It's just ... Jeez, I dunno. The things you two stress over.'

'Like what?'

'Your lives!' Bridget stared into the sink. 'Oh no. I broke a plate.'

'Don't worry,' said Ebony, 'we'll do the dishes.'

'I gotta go anyway,' Bridget said.

The sounds of the television intruded. The Sunday musical tap-danced into the room, at odds with the tense mood.

Ebony's forehead creased. 'Bridget? Oh crap, you're bleeding.'

Bridget stared at her hand as crimson drops fell to the tiled floor, splattering carelessly. She seemed to be mesmerised by the sight. She slashed a hand across her damp forehead.

The storm outside exploded. The pale strobe of the television flashed and jarred down the hallway into the darkening room.

Turning slowly towards the girls, Bridget lifted her gaze. Then, her eyes rolled back as her body went limp.

Jenna lunged and broke her fall.

Ebony screamed, then called out. 'Dad! Emma!'

The house buzzed, shocked from Sunday bliss as Brady scooped Bridget up and carried her to the lounge room, where he lay her on the sofa.

'Throw me a tea towel, Eb—something to ... thanks Jenna.' Emma balled the tea towel and held it on Bridget's hand.

'I'll ... get a facecloth,' said Ebony, 'a wet one.' She was rewarded with a grateful look from Emma.

'Put her feet up Brady,' said Emma. She palpated the pulse at the base of the girl's pale wrist, now exposed as the gauzy sleeves of the shirt were free, revealing scars on Bridget's forearm. She flipped the cuffs back down as she took the cool cloth from Ebony.

Ebony blanched at the sight, and stumbled back into Jenna.

Bridget's lashes fluttered. She moaned softly as Emma's words intruded. Then her eyes opened in alarm. She sat up, her breathing hard and fast.

'You fainted, Bridget,' said Emma, placing a hand on her shoulder, 'you might need to lie down for...'

Bridget put her hand over her mouth as harsh sobs fought to escape. 'No! Leave me! Alone!'

'Just let me dress the...'

Emma's hand was thrust aside as Bridget ran. Down the hall and out the front door.

'Bridget!' Jenna's voice was torn.

'What the hell?' Brady turned confused eyes on the girls.

'We have to go after her, Dad.' Ebony was already out the door, carrying a jade throw she'd grabbed off the lounge.

Brady and the girls checked the track through the bushland.

Emma drove the short distance to Bridget's home. There was no sign of the girl on the road. The car tyres spewed gravel on the driveway to the rundown Galloway house. The gloom of the place permeated the air. Emma rapped on the decaying screen door, and peered into the dark interior. A metallic clunk answered. Smoke from the wood heater that was lit on even the warmest day stifled the room.

Bridget's father appeared. He held a beer can and a cigarette in his left hand and gripped the large timber door with his right hand, opening it mere inches.

'I'm not buyin' nuthin',' he said, relishing a long drag on the cigarette, as he blew the smoke into Emma's face. He chuckled, and that liberty brought on a fit of coughing.

'I'm not a sales rep, Mr Galloway.' Emma paused, conscious of the character of the man in front of her. Bridget didn't deserve this. 'Is Bridget around?'

'Nah, she's prob'ly off with those stuck-up friends of 'ers. Right little misses they are. Not that it's any of your bus'ness, Miss, what's yer name?'

'Emma Harcourt.'

'Huh! That community nurse. Poking yer nose in are yer? Well, on yer bike darlin'. You got no truck pushing in ter our affairs. We don't need no welfare types.' The door closed a fraction. 'Ere, I tell yer wot—if yer do find 'er, tell 'er to get 'erself home ter cook me tea. Ta rah. Shove orf. Whatcha waitin' fer? Forms in triplicate? Ha Ha!'

The door slammed. Emma looked around. She remembered the place. The old man had broken his arm and been referred to the community nurses several years ago. He'd made short work of the girl who had come to see him.

The yard was littered with the usual accoutrements of a home that had once sustained life, but now contained only the detritus of that existence. An axe protruded awkwardly from a large block of wood, stuck there, probably left in a drunken stupor. Or maybe Tom Galloway was making some kind of point to the universe. He'd worked in the timber yard until he'd been sacked for operating machinery under the influence of alcohol. His wife had left a year later, although according to Galloway's version of events, it was her leaving that had unravelled his life.

Emma waited in the car for a few minutes. When there was no sign of Bridget, she returned to join Brady and the girls in the search.

They found Bridget an hour later, cold and trembling, curled into a hollowed tree trunk. Dead branches of the blue gum pointed to the dark sky, where thunder threatened with dull Thor rumblings, and lightning shards flowered earthwards in the distance.

The storm was spent, and so was Bridget. Her eyes were wild, her body jerked. Ebony wrapped the throw around her.

Brady lifted Bridget into his arms. 'We must get her father.'

'No!' Ebony and Jenna shouted.

Brady looked to Emma.

Emma shook her head. 'We'll take Bridget to A&E at the hospital. I'll phone ahead. She shouldn't be there long. A few blood tests. IV fluids will sort her out.'

'Can we come?' Ebony's eyes were taut with anxiety.

'I guess,' said Brady, seeking Emma's approval with his eyes.

'Sure,' said Emma, 'but you won't be able to go in with her. I'll take her in. You'll have to sit in the outpatients waiting area.' Emma stroked Bridget's face as Brady put her into the car. 'I want to get her home as soon as possible.'

'But, home is the problem,' said Jenna. 'Make a report or something, can't you?'

'I know you girls worry about Bridget. Her home life is problematic. We will do all we can.'

Brady carried the limp girl into the A&E. A nurse ushered

them into the examination area.

Ebony scanned the waiting room. Prudence Wainwright's friend, Adeline Court was watching the scene intently. Ebony moaned. That meant Mrs Wainwright, and the school, would be notified. And interfere. Again. Busybodies, the lot of them.

Fluorescent lights stuttered. Bridget cowered under a white sheet. Her rail thin body was poignantly evident. She had remonstrated against being brought in, but fainting for the second time put paid to her resolution. As much as she would have liked the company of Jenna and Ebony they had been vetoed.

'I can't stay here,' muttered Bridget, 'Da will be ... I have to get home.'

'You're really dehydrated, love. You need some IV fluids. That won't take long. The doctor has ordered it. You fainted twice, you know. Right out to it. I need to phone someone, can you give me the number.'

Bridget's voice came out in a gravely whisper, 'You can't ... you just can't...'

'Is there a problem, love? According to your date of birth, you're sixteen yeah? You're a minor pet, we prefer to have permission.'

'Yes. Sixteen! You can't make me stay.' Bridget sat up quickly. The room spun wildly, as the pale girl plomped back on the narrow trolley in the corridor.

The nurse puckered her lips. 'Honey we just want to get you hydrated, okay. So once this IV is empty we'll let you go. It will only take an hour to go through. You're right, we don't have to talk to anyone if you don't want, but it would be best to have an adult in here with you. Is there anyone else?'

'Emma, the woman who brought me in—is she still here?'

'I can see for you. But let's get you into a cubicle, and onto a bed.'

The nurse steered the trolley down the hall. The curtain slid aside with a mechanical whir as the nurse flicked it back and wheeled Bridget into a private cubicle. Deftly pulling the curtain across, the nurse placed a cotton blanket over the girl.

'What's the name of the woman?'

'Emma Harcourt.'

'Ah right. The community nurse.'

However, it wasn't Emma who was ushered in. It was Byron. Bridget was so relieved she cried. 'How'd you know I was here?'

'Sources,' said Byron.

'You sound like Jenna.'

'Your mouthy friend? Shoot me now. Anyway sis, you'd better keep still so the nurse can find a vein.'

'Thanks,' said the nurse, flicking the back of Bridget's hand.

'Just look at me, Bridgee,' Byron said, reaching for her hand. 'Be over in a jiff. Then I can take you home.'

Back in the ramshackle house, Bridget slept all night and late into the next day. A rhythmic creaking of floorboards woke her. With her senses on instant alert she looked through a slim crack in the door.

It was Byron.

Bridget threw open the door and hugged him.

'Whoa, you okay sis?'

'Just glad to see you. Bridget combed her fingers through

straggly hair. 'Where's Da?'

Byron chuckled. 'Oh, he's still out for the count. He'll probably be down for a while yet.'

'That's suspicious, but I don't want to know. What's the time?'

'You still don't have a phone? That's bonkers. Every kid has one.'

'Pfft.' Bridget blew air through tight lips and thumped her brother's arm. 'Well, it's like this, dear brother, I don't have an income, don't have pocket money, blah blah. However, I do have a loving brother who happens to sell mobile phones and I just had my 16th birthday, celebrated at the town cem...' a sigh, Bridget gritted her teeth, to hold back tears.

'Oh fuck, sis, I didn't think. I'm sorry.' Byron chewed the corner of his mouth. 'Crap, wait a minute.' He reached into a coat pocket. 'I'm late with your birthday present. Can you forgive me?'

He produced a slim white box. 'Er, sorry it's not wrapped. Here come sit at the table and I'll go over how it works.'

'But Da...'

'He'll be out for hours. Honestly. He might be starving when he wakes up thought. Salt, he'll want salt. I, um shared a toke with him last night. Mellowed him right down. He didn't even ask where you were? Ordered pizza for tea. He right wolfed that down. You shoulda seen the old dude.'

'He's ... oh, it's much better when you're here.'

The pain in his sister's eyes gave Byron a pang of guilt. It was testament to his sister's good nature that she never tossed blame his way. Most kids would and that made him feel worse.

He didn't know what to say so he started to open the box, which was swiftly grabbed by Bridget.

'Let me. I never have new stuff.'

Byron's face relaxed. He went through the basics, Bridget caught on quickly.

After the lesson was over Bridget noticed a large gym bag in the hall. 'Oh good, you're staying? That's one heck of a bag, you must have enough clothes to start your own men's store.'

Byron cleared his throat, 'Um yeah. Well, a few days anyway. I'm, between flats. Anyway, have fun with your new phone. Remember that it's only prepaid.'

'Yeah, you said already.'

Before Byron left, he set up his stuff in the sunroom at the back of the house.

Bridget closed her window. Put the kerosene lamp in the small cupboard by the bed. No need to escape while Byron was home.

It was 11.00 am. Too late for school. She hadn't been sure if she was going anyway. She wanted to avoid any confrontation with Mrs Busybody Wainwright after her hospital stay. She didn't want to repeat that exercise, well, both really, Mrs Wainwright and the A&E incident. The doctor had expressed concern over her fainting and had mentioned electrolytes. She'd have to sneak that on the grocery list Carol managed. She should be grateful to the woman. If she didn't eavesdrop on their conversations she wouldn't know a thing.

God knows why Da didn't accept government help for that sort of thing. He had a Gold card for goodness sake. He was happy to get a town car to take him to medical appointments.

Bridget prepared a salty lunch for Da and went to the cemetery shack to play with the phone.

Byron had taken out the sim card, replacing it with a new one, which made her suspicious that the phone hadn't been intended for her, but what the heck. She had a phone. And there was $50 credit. She'd have to make it last.

She couldn't wait to show Jenna and Ebony. They would be half way through a boring day at school.

Or so she thought.

Mrs Wainwright had indeed heard of Bridget's visit to the local A&E and was determined to carry out her version of a Welfare Check. Unable to find Bridget, she called Ebony Harcourt in, considered to be the quietest of the trio. The compliant one.

Which was usually correct, but not on this day.

'What! Excuse me!' Ebony stood by the filing cabinet, fists clenched. Heat rose in her face, darkening her pale complexion.

'It's alright, Ebony. We deal with these things all the time. We want you to trust us.' The woman stood. She took a step towards Ebony and reached out a hand. 'We are just concerned about your, um, little Goth friend. The um, weekend trouble you girls had that landed, um,' Prudence Wainwright looked down, 'Bridget, yes, that's right, Bridget Galloway. In hospital.'

'Who told you?'

'Ebony, dear.'

'This is not school business. Our privacy has been invaded.'

'Ebony, there's no need ... we ... ah, they have your best

interests ... They told us in confidence...'

'Oh, bloody marvellous, that is. "They" being the faceless experts everyone calls on to validate their story.'

Mrs Wainwright, temp school counsellor, blanched and took a step back. She had been seriously misinformed. Wait till she saw that sweet-faced English teacher who had ushered Ebony in after a whispered phrase behind her hand that Ebony Harcourt was a "shy little thing". But a casual introduction to the girl and a bland opening sentence of 'we heard that you girls had some trouble over the weekend...' had raised the girl's hackles. That itself was a most unsatisfactory piece of information, apparently just a piece of the whole, and then she had made the tactical mistake of relying on the observations of her friend Adeline's encyclopaedic knowledge of local affairs. A circumstance she now regretted. It was Adeline who'd informed her of Bridget's hospitalisation as if it was a major event, something that she now realised could get her into trouble with the school, much less little Madam Ebony Harcourt.

Retreat seemed the best option. 'I didn't bring you here to put you on the mat,' she said, attempting to stand tall, quite an aspiration for a short busty woman. 'We were ... '

The door flew open, startling both occupants. It was the teacher who had brought Ebony. 'Sorry Mrs Wainwright. I just wanted thought I'd let you know that we are rounding up the other girls.' She handed the woman a scrap of paper.

This sentence, although it was delivered with the warmest of smiles had an alarming effect on Ebony, and brought no joy to Mrs Wainwright who now had an investment in quelling the whole affair.

'Hell,' said Ebony, marching towards the door, forcing Mrs Wainwright to turn. As she did, the glare of the sun through the window caught her full in the face. She blinked and held up a hand.

'Well Ebony, it seems, erm that everything is in order… if you don't want to talk about it,' she said, vainly attempting to hide her sense of injury, 'you don't have to.'

'Damned straight I don't.'

Mrs Wainwright was perplexed. After that outburst she'd expected the girl to flounce out of the room, an event that would have greatly improved her assessment of the situation, but the little minx had taken a seat in the worn, boxy two-seater under the window, that had been installed to put students at ease. This action further discomforted the already tense woman whose sole desire was for Ebony to leave, any way she chose to do so. The slanted sunlight was now relentless. She struggled to focus.

'Ebony,' Mrs Wainwright felt around behind her for a chair, 'we should talk to, er,' She consulted the piece of paper in her hand and read 'Jenna … um Bragg, and Bridget Galloway herself of course.'

'NO way in hell!' Ebony stood abruptly, narrowly missing Mrs Wainwright's searching arc for the chair. 'Stay away from Bridget. You hear me. Stay. Away. From. Bridget Galloway.'

Mrs Wainwright's skin paled against her puce green suit. A hand flew to her throat where a pulse thudded in the soft folds of her several chins. 'But dear…'

Ebony let out a long sigh and wiped her eyes. She hadn't

meant to be angry, certainly not this angry, and with the one person who could shine a focus on Bridget. It could tip the fragile girl over the edge. The fact that their frail friend needed help had not escaped Ebony and Jenna. But this awkward interfering? She'd seen that old crow Adeline at the A&E and expected something.

Ebony looked at the door in the tense silence, but to leave now would only draw more attention to Bridget. She stole a glance at Mrs Wainwright and realised the women was as uncomfortable as she was. The powdered lines of the woman's face conveyed anxiety and a little fear.

Outrage would gain no ground here.

Ebony quickly wiped a tear. She cursed her weakness until she saw that Mrs Wainwright's face had changed. For the better. 'Mrs Wainwright, you don't understand, you see. We were not mucking up on the weekend. We were searching for my grandmother. She'd gone missing. She has dementia and wanders off. Grandie does a great job of looking after her, but she slipped out when he thought she was having a nap. Jenna and Bridget helped us search, even though it was late.' Ebony yawned for effect. She had to carry off this lie. 'Poor Bridget um, got caught on a barbed wire fence, yes, and she had to, um, have a dressing. So you see it's all nothing. I'm sorry I was angry, Mrs Wainwright. I've been having...' Ebony nearly choked on the words, 'a bit of stress lately.'

'Don't cry dear. It's alright. We can get you some help.'

'I have a counsellor, Mrs Wainwright. I do. Ah, er ... Dad has found a really good one. Ah ...' Ebony saw Mrs Wainwright's hand reach for a pen. 'Ah. She's in the city, um, you wouldn't have heard of her. Um, she knew our family, ah, before…,' Ebony felt her throat constricting. She stepped closer to the door. She had to get out of the place. 'And, she's really good. Thanks for caring, goodbye.'

Mrs Wainwright stared at the closed door. 'Good heavens,' she said. She looked at the clock on the wall. 'Thank God I'm only filling in, this is a right madhouse.'

Prudence Wainwright found the confines of the small office suddenly claustrophobic. The prospect of further student interviews filled her with a dread she hadn't known since she'd worked in the city. A quick perusal of the appointment diary on the desk showed there were no more scheduled appointments for the day. That left "walk ins". There was a discomforting unpredictability to "walk ins" that she had not foreseen or been forewarned about when she arrived for her casual week's work. A brief wave of the Welfare Teacher's hand and a dismissive, 'you've only got walk-ins to worry about–that's kids who come to say hello or because one of the teachers has referred them for a bit of a chat. They won't be a problem because the kids have agreed to come happily'.

Prudence Wainwright felt betrayed. Ms Ebony Harcourt had not been a "walk in".

Prudence had always felt that discretion was the better part of valour. This philosophy had held her in good stead in her previous employment, even if that was twenty years ago. It took her several minutes of pacing in her shiny black court shoes before she came up with a satisfactory solution. Old Habits die hard, so Prudence resorted to past tactics. "When in trouble, look busy". With a load of folders gripped under her ample arm she set off on a brisk walk down the corridors.

Only vaguely familiar with the layout, she was not deterred and shortly found herself outside the library, which was blissfully devoid of students of any description, so she settled herself at a remote desk, straight-backed and professional, and began to peruse the folders.

She heaved a deep and audible sigh when she realised what the folders contained, they were devoted to a subject she found even more repellent than students—cooking. Damn and blast.

Shock

Prudence Wainwright adjusted her sunglasses. Normally she considered the wearing of sunglasses in a café as pretentious, but she wanted some peace and quiet, and at her age she could always plead sensitive eyes. Peace and quiet. It was unbelievable the number of people who came to her with gossip. For the life of her, she couldn't see why. Today she just wanted to read a magazine, have a frothy cappuccino, and watch the world go by. She'd had an early morning sherry to fortify herself for the day. Thank God she didn't have to go to the school.

As long as she didn't see Emma Harcourt, the clinic nurse—the step-mother of that outrageous child Ebony, she'd be fine. The memory of the girl's tirade still stung. And she knew better than to tackle Emma Harcourt. That step-mother was more protective than even a biological mother had a right to be.

Maybe she was getting too old for the school job. It wasn't as if they needed the money. Earl was very successful as town planner. Well respected too. They were invited to all the best social engagements. It was a bit tiring at times, but one must do one's community duty. It was a shame they hadn't had children. Earl had been disappointed; he'd have made a good father.

Prudence had worked very hard over the years to fill the gap in every possible way. He hadn't been partial to the youth programs so she felt that he surely didn't miss fatherhood. Their uncomplicated life allowed him to pursue his career and there was no denying that their status in the community was a boon. She was very proud of him. After all, everyone knew that behind every good man was a good woman. Why he'd just been elected Mayor. Their affluence, if one should call it that, did allow her some little indulgences to make up for his long hours and work commitments.

Originally glad to be out of the sun and humidity, Prudence was beginning to be bored. This was the best café in town, but honestly the service was slow. Today was her special day out. Every week she went all out on a hairdo and lunch. Normally she would have read a magazine or had a coffee before Adeline arrived, but today she was unaccountably tetchy.

What on earth was keeping Adeline? The one day she could do with some company and Addy was late. Not that Prudence called her that, she abhorred any abbreviations to names people were given. She looked at her watch. Adeline must have been caught up chatting to someone. That was the only drawback with her friend. She was a bit of a gossip, and Prudence was not in favour of that sort of thing.

Reaching for the menu for the hundredth time, Prudence

consoled herself with the fact that she would feel so much better after her hair appointment. It gave her such a lift.

Looking out of the café window she saw a young woman with gorgeous red hair. Well, it would have been gorgeous if it had been tamed a little. But the colour, it was stunning. It was exactly the colour of Prudence's when she was young. She sighed. All the dye and pampering in the world had not managed to return her hair to its former glory. Life just wasn't fair.

Having nothing better to do, Prudence watched the girl. She seemed to be pouring over a map of some sort, occasionally looking up at the shops. Then she picked up a large woven basket with two long handles, not unlike a carpet bag, and crossed the road. She was heading for the café. A waiter jumped up to help her in the door. Oh dear, you could hardly see the girl for that wild mane.

'S'cuse me, Miss. I've been told a Mrs Prudence Wainwright is in this café. Could you please point her out if she's here?' The girl waved a grubby piece of paper.

Prudence blanched and sunk behind the menu. What on earth could this hippy person want with her? She hoped it wasn't a council matter. It was one of her pet hates when people seemed to hold her accountable for Earl's development decisions. Looking up, she was horrified to see the waitress directing the girl to her table.

'Look, my dear, if this is something to do with a council deci...' Prudence stopped dead. A carbon copy of her face at twenty was looking back at her. Except for those brown eyes...

'Hello, Mum. I betcha never expected me to find you. It was such a bloody struggle to get anywhere with that awful adoption agency woman. It was just real lucky for us that you arranged a private adoption, and I found that lovely old duck from the church that took care of it all ... Oh dear, are y'all right?'

Prudence heard a buzzing in her head. The room spun. There was a strange voice penetrating the fuzziness.

'Quick, put her head down. She's going to faint.' She felt someone hold her head between her legs. 'Could you get Prudence some water, love,' said Adeline Baker. 'She's going to pass out.' The waitress and Adeline Baker insisted she lie down on the bench seat.

A baby cried. The strange girl picked a tiny infant out of the carry all, and soothed it. The baby had no nappy. The basket was lined with an old towel.

'Shush, now, bub. Yer grandmother isn't well.'

Annabel took this news with little interest, and screamed louder.

'Oh, crikey! Do you think she'll pass out?' asked the girl.

Please God, I wish, thought Prudence Wainwright.

It was her last thought as everything went black, although she was later heard to say that there was a beautiful light in the distance, beckoning her. It wouldn't do for anyone to think that she, Prudence Wainwright, had missed out on an 'other-worldly' experience. Why they might think she was without redemption.

While the world stopped then for the unconscious Prudence Wainwright, chaos reigned around her. An ambulance was called. A crowd gathered.

Willow Brown, Prudence's visitor, and newly discovered daughter, organised the crowd with calm self-assurance. No one dared argue with this confident carbon-copy of Prudence. Her lineage was accepted without question.

Someone phoned Earl's secretary and informed him of what had happened. A temp covering for Earl's long-time assistant, the new girl calmly accepted the presence of a daughter in her boss's life. After all, he was an intensely private man and she hadn't had time for office gossip, she'd been too busy working out the basics of her job and too nervous to ask the other staff for information. She noticed the colour drain from his face at the news. Then, grabbing his coat, he rushed out of the office without a word.

Another office worker, tapped into the local grapevine, and sensing a monetary reward from the newspapers, phoned and tipped them off, so that when Earl arrived at the local public hospital, cameras were flashing from all directions outside the Accident and Emergency Ward.

He was confronted by a strange girl who looked the spitting image of Prudence around the time he met her. This garrulous new person had already gained validity as Prudence's only child, and was holding court with the press. She gave a detailed account of the terrible health crisis of her newly-found mother, adding a gentle sniff and a well-timed tear or two.

Earl's customary presence of mind completely deserted him in the face of such inexplicable circumstances. All he could do was stutter.

When the basket Willow was carrying let out a loud howl, the staff were shocked beyond belief, as she had travelled in the ambulance to the hospital. The infant hadn't been restrained.

The A&E supervisor cornered the ambulance driver, a paramedic.

The paramedic couldn't remember being more embarrassed when he was asked by a gathering of journalists why he'd done something so reckless and against the law. The explanation that he thought the young woman merely had a rather large tatty carryall didn't seem adequate, so with his best authoritative voice he said, 'Step aside, will you lot! There's a very ill woman here.'

The supervisor decided that discretion was indeed the better part of valour. With a growing audience he stepped in to part the crowd of journalists to allow the ambulance men to push the trolley with an unconscious Prudence Wainwright through the patient entrance. Then he ushered Earl and Willow through the glass doors to the Accident and Emergency waiting room, where a burly hospital security man had been hastily called to guard the door.

A&E

In the next cubicle to Prudence Wainwright, Byron Galloway, overdose victim and alcohol poisoning patient in Bed 4, made a conscious effort to relax, as the nurse organising his transfer to the ward swished the curtain across in a vain attempt at privacy for the new admission.

After being in the emergency room for 10 hours the worst of Byron's hallucinations were over, although things were still a bit hazy. The place was pandemonium, staff bustling everywhere. Some old duck had had "an event". Some politician's wife, he'd gathered that much—he'd overheard 'mayor. The woman was getting instant attention. Two nurses were asking questions and discussing obs, as machines were wheeled in and out. Through the gap in the curtain he saw a different doctor to the one he'd had, attending to the woman and giving the nurses permission to let family in.

Then the old bird's husband arrived. He was followed by a weird orange-haired hippy woman with a squalling baby, who was asked to sit in the waiting area. She protested like mad, saying she was the woman's daughter. The noise level went through the roof. It was a right circus. Byron strained to see, but it was all a blur of activity. Staff were running round like mad, ranting about the media. Lots of media, apparently. Even though they were in the waiting area their presence could be heard.

Byron was alert then. If he hadn't been a patient himself the whole thing would have amused him. Apparently the old bird had adopted a kid out a thousand years ago—must be the orange-haired hippy. So Mr VIP Mayor, had arrived to discover that not only was his wife on the brink of death, she had a secret daughter, and a grandkid. That conversation had been very enlightening. The hippy woman was a loud piece of work. The staff and ambos hadn't been impressed, and God only knows what the VIP made of it all. Someone would have their work cut out to put a positive spin on this lot. Byron bristled at the unfairness of it all. The politician would come out of it squeaky clean. They got all the breaks, and he'd be treated like a criminal.

He heard the name Prudence Wainwright, he certainly knew her. Everyone in Noarlunga knew the mayor's busybody wife. He'd even been cornered by her a few times himself. He shuddered at the thought. The nurses thought they were whispering, assuming he was too far gone to understand. He smirked as he was wheeled away from the chaos to the ward.

He was shocked to be put in a four-bed women's ward, but was too grateful for the sedative he was given to offset the effects of the alcohol in his system to care.

Byron felt a light touch on his shoulder. A headless Benji weaved around the room, blood spurting. There was a dark shadow following him. It must be the grim reaper, come for him.

He shuddered awake. He must have drifted off. Shit, what a nightmare. Thank goodness he didn't have reactions like that all the time. He'd give the stuff up in a heartbeat. He remembered a friend's saying about hash. 'It's like a good looking woman who doesn't have to offer you anything. You know you want her. You know she'll break your balls and suck the soul right out of you; but you still want to have her.'

The mother of all headaches was cracking his skull open. His stomach felt like he had been stampeded by a herd of elephants, from the numerous hurling episodes of last night. He must have been ripped out of his mind.

With only a thin curtain between them, the crackling wheeze from the patient in the next bed sounded like a car backfiring. If that old bag made that whistling bloody noise again Byron would go and kill her himself. So, she was dying. So what! Everyone died. Everything had a beginning and an end. It was her time to go, that's all. Why the hell was she in this fucking last place in earth you wanted to be, hospital ward? Weren't there hospices for this sort of thing?

One thing was certain—this wasn't going to happen to him again. You had to make a mistake to learn from it and he was no idiot. He'd never buy his stash from that lowlife, pisshead Benji again. What sort of a fucked up name was Benji anyway. But even as he vowed to ditch Benji, the memory of the hash in his gym bag at the house made him nervous. He was playing for higher stakes now–selling small amounts to friends he trusted. He shuddered as he wondered if anyone else had found the latest stuff a bit strong.

Shit, that was the only part of this whole business he hated. The insecurity of the quality of the gear. They should get it right, the dickheads. He laughed ironically at his own train of thought. Quality Control, Occupation Health & Safety courses for dealers. Yeah right!

Not that he thought of Benji as a 'dealer'—he was a supplier. A supplier of a service that was just misunderstood. Illegal and misunderstood. It made him angry. Especially now that he had a few kilos stashed at the old man's house. He would never call that place home. He should have been in a condo on the beach by now, would have if he hadn't lost his job. His boss had tossed him like a piece of garbage. So he'd had a bad month, everyone in sales had those. He'd tried to explain that he was stuck with his old man who was really ill, but Dave didn't buy it. Guess everyone in this town knew his father was a good-for-nothing drunk.

Byron would not have admitted, even to himself that he'd started smoking in the morning, at lunch time and again at the end of every day. To keep him calm. To get to sleep. To get him through to the next day. It was no different than going to the doc to get something to help him calm down, chill out.

Why did government health authorities ban something that had less evidence of harm than tobacco smoking? Why hell, if they would come out of the closet and tell him just what their story was, show the compelling body of indisputable evidence that put marijuana off the legal list, why he'd be the first to believe and give it up.

They hadn't banned tobacco even though they paid huge bucks to advertise its harmful effects. If it was as bad as they said it was then why didn't they get off their collective legislating arses and outlaw it, arrest people and be done with it? Put their money where their mouth was. That was probably what it all came down to anyway, money.

The wheeze in the next bed turned into a rattle that echoed on every side of his skull. Jesus, he couldn't take much more of this.

'Sorry, Son,' said a feeble voice. Oh shit, he must have said it out loud. He pushed the pillow around his ears and groaned. Oh shit. For the first time in that interminable day he felt sorry for someone other than himself. Poor silly old bitch wasn't dying just to annoy him.

'Didn't mean to be rude, lady,' he grumbled reluctantly. 'I just have a headache that would split concrete and I've hurled all night.'

'That's dreadful,' responded the voice behind the curtain. 'Why don't you ring the nurse and ask for something? Can I help?'

Oh Jeez, sympathy from the dying now. This had to be his worst day on earth.

'Yeah well,' he said with a half-hearted chuckle, 'they aren't likely to do that as my present problem came about because of a little too much medication already, if you get my drift.'

'Oh, I see, you hit the bottle and it hit you back.' Her voice was so soft he could hardly catch what she was saying.

'Bit like that,' he said dismissively. He rolled over noisily, making the hospital bed squeak, hoping she would take the hint.

She didn't speak again. Well, maybe she was dead. He suddenly thought how horrible it would be to be a few feet away from someone when they died. Jeez, get me out of here, he thought. Then the crackling wheeze began again and he breathed a sigh of relief.

The nurse came in. It was the skinny blonde with the big laugh. Melda or Melody or something. She'd introduced herself to the two of them a few hours ago. Chatted away like a bloody cheerful parrot she had. What sort of people were nurses anyway? Walking into rooms with people taking their last breath, and idiots like him who had accidentally overdosed, and treating them as if they were all at some god-dammed Wiggles concert.

The nurse flicked the curtain back with a swoosh. The metal curtain rings sounded like screaming metal. He moaned.

'Is your head still bad,' she said sympathetically. 'Do you want me to get you something for it?'

'Didn't think I could have anything,' he muttered. 'Thought you people didn't give dope addicts anything? You think we deserve our suffering for being fucking idiots.'

'Slight paranoia creeping in, Byron. Are you a dope addict?' she asked, with a teasing smile. She tilted her head to the side as she looked at him. Wow! She was a stunner up close.

'No, I'm not,' he denied defensively.

'Never touch the stuff, huh?' she folded her arms across the nursing notes on the plastic clipboard. God he wished she would stop talking and trying to make him think. His head pounded.

'I didn't say that. I know what you lot think but there is a huge difference between a dope addict and a recreational user.'

Byron sat up in the bed to lessen the feeling that the girl had a towering advantage over him. He felt a bit overwhelmed by this cool, good-looking chick. He must look like the bottom of a fish bowl.

'Ah, so you're a fucking idiot.' She held his gaze. 'Your words, not mine.'

'Oh, so that's my official diagnosis, is it nurse?' He was angry now.

'It's like this Byron. There is a huge difference between the official diagnosis and the real diagnosis.'

'You're pretty uptight about it. You nurses like the stuff as much as the rest of us. I've seen plenty of you smoking weed.'

'Sounds like you have quite a body of evidence for an occasional user,' she mocked.

'Yeah well,' he spat out, 'more evidence that you medical fucking experts can come up with.' He snorted, realising that he was making a poor show of himself. He wished she would go away, she was better to look at than to listen to.

She laughed. 'I'll bring you something as soon as I've given Helena her nebuliser.'

'That's what they all say,' he whined.

What was it with her? She was still cheerful, while he felt so wound up he could spit nails. With deft expert hands she undid the tubing of the nebulizer and filled the small receptacle on the mask with a plastic ampoule from a metal tray. He was in awe at her ease with it all. How good would it be if you could get your gear that easily. Just line up for it. No phone calls, no sly meetings avoiding cops or prying eyes. There'd be no relying on mates or dodgy idiots, who acted like they'd known you forever merely because you shared a laugh over a spliff, and they claimed to know where to get the best hash.

He sunk back into the bed, suddenly exhausted from the mental effort of talking. Grateful that the nurse had pulled the curtain, Byron tried to relax. At least the thin curtain might stop the woman in the bed next to him from yakking. It had discomforted him no end when she'd casually mentioned that her husband was a private investigator.

Just as he thought he might actually drift off, the woman had visitors. Two teenage girls. Through the gap in the curtain he saw that one of them was a blonde piece he'd chatted up on the train. The one who'd pretended to be deaf and humiliated him. Anger rose until he wanted to punch something, or someone. He turned over slowly and pulled the sheet above his head.

'Thanks for coming Jenna sweetheart,' said the woman, 'and Ebony. How did you get here?'

'Rode our bikes. Dad got one for our friend. Through the Youth Program. Can you believe it's her first bike, Helena?'

The blonde's voice was grating. A real chatty type. He'd heard her mother was an actor. Well the girl had inherited that gene. Why was she here visiting the woman? Small towns, I hate them, he thought. Everyone knows your business. If I could, I'd be tempted to up stakes and move on. Like Mum did.

'Has Dad been in today?' asked the blonde.

Byron froze. The blonde was the daughter of the local P.I?

It wasn't exactly a connection to the cops, but it was too close for comfort. Life was certainly conspiring against him.

Paranoia set in as Byron thought of his stash. It was safer in his wardrobe at his father's rundown place. The old dude might be a useless drunk but he sure knew how to send the cops packing.

There was silence in the room. Byron realised the girls had gone while he'd been stressing about the past.

Where was that nurse with his pain relief? He'd never needed anything more.

He couldn't wait to be out of the place. He would have signed himself out, but that would gain more attention. He'd just be quiet and polite. Benji was the only one who knew about his stash and not even he knew where it was hidden. He was safe. He couldn't let paranoia get the better of him.

The wheeze from the woman had eased. There was now the whirr of a nebuliser machine. At least she had peace. Even Byron, in his selfish state of mind, could wish her that. The whoosh of the mist she was sucking in seemed as precious as God's own breath, straight to her.

Byron wondered briefly what had happened to the Mayor's wife, busybody Mrs Wainwright. She'd been in the A&E ward next to him. With a secret daughter, and a screeching baby. Ha. There was some justice in life. Mr Mayor had scandal on his own door now.

Welcome to the real world, Grandpa.

Musing

The object of Byron's musings was in a private room on the general ward. While she should have been grateful the transfer from the busy A&E, Prudence Wainwright was engaged with musings of her own. Assisted with a hefty dose of morphine she abandoned her stiff persona and wandered lightly back into the past.

As soon as she'd looked beyond the likeness of her younger self in her daughter, she had seen the rich brown eyes of an AmEarlan soldier who'd served in Vietnam. What a beautiful man he'd been–Willow's father. Wounded inside and out, Chuck Reise had awakened a powerful longing in Prudence. For the first time in her life she was needed, desired. She set out to heal his suffering in the age-old manner of besotted women the world over; in bed. Or was it a bunk–isn't that what he'd called the tiny bench on the ship where he'd taken her willingly offered virginity?

Apparently it had healed him, she thought, with not a small

measure of bitterness, for he was gone in days; with not a word or a backward glance. But he had left something behind. A child. The one gift she'd been unable to give to dear Earl, who would have made the best of fathers. Earl, the meticulous man who noticed her quiet reserve in the solicitor's office where she had worked. All those years ago.

To all appearances Prudence had managed to reinvent herself after the birth of the child and the adoption. When she gained a position at a prestigious law firm she had forbidden any shortening of her name. The Prue of the past was gone. Her floral prints were replaced with stern suits, with just a modest cowl neck to soften the look. She wore her hair up, coiled tightly in a barrette. Not a wisp was allowed to stray. She would never be a plaything again.

Earl had been a fresh-faced junior partner in those days. He was five years younger than her—just a 'pup'. Beside him, she felt jaded and wounded. Until he asked her out.

He'd been persistent in those days–intrigued by her. The shadow of sorrow she wore translated as something else, something he wanted. Prudence Drago had never been pursued–she'd been needed and yes, desired, but not sought after like a prize. He never looked at the office beauties with their carefree party lifestyles. He wanted her. She'd intended to tell him about the child, the hasty adoption her mother had organised, but things had moved so quickly. Before she had even formed her own feelings, Earl had gone down on one knee.

The right time had never come.

Hot tears scalded her eyes and she blinked them back. She would not cry, not now. But dear God, what would she lose? Everything she had so patiently worked for? Her husband? Her home? It didn't bear thinking about, but there it was—gnawing at her like an abscessed tooth.

She loved Earl. Not with the desperate passion that had swept her away in her youth with the American, but with friendship, warmth and gratitude. She determined to become everything she thought he wanted, charting an ambitious course to status. At first it had been for Earl, but somewhere along the way it had become about her. She was a valued asset, a woman of substance. How often she'd prided herself on achieving the precise life she'd always wanted, a life far from her humble roots. But now, in one fell swoop, all of that was in jeopardy, unravelling before her eyes.

If only the meeting with her daughter hadn't been so public. If only she hadn't taken a turn and ended up the centre of a media circus. If only she hadn't allowed her mother to arrange a private adoption; expedient at the time. This one factor made the way clear for her daughter to find her.

If only she'd had time to prepare Earl. Dear Earl. How would he react? He had brought security and reliability into her life. He'd given her the dream life she had striven so hard to attain. Earl had been so grateful when she'd welcomed their relocation from the city to Noarlunga, never knowing her relief that the move would distance her even further from the past. A new town had delivered the safety she craved, and with Earl's involvement in the community and rise to prominence in the council, she'd become a real part of the place.

In an instant her world had tilted. It was too late to go back. It was impossible to go forward. While the baby she'd only glanced at in the delivery room remained a shadowy figure in the past, she had almost been able to convince herself that none of it had happened. But now that shadow was real. There would be questions—questions she didn't want to think about, much less answer. There was only one certainty—life as she knew it had changed forever.

Pain cramped her chest and she moaned softly. She reached for the call bell. She might not be able to escape the past, but she didn't need the physical pain of the present. A Sister arrived.

'What can I do for you, Mrs Wainwright? Is it the pain?'

Prudence nodded.

The Sister checked her watch, and smiled. Patting Prudence's hand she said, 'You're doing well. I'll get you something. You're due.'

The sister returned and inserted a needle into the IV cannula. She watched Prudence clenching her hands together.

'Just breathe slowly, Mrs Wainwright. You've been through a lot. You'll need a procedure. An angiogram. To check the flow to your heart. There'll be an anaesthetic. They want to rule out permanent damage. The specialist explained that, didn't he?'

'Yes,' said Prudence, flinching at the word 'permanent' and feeling guilty that she hadn't paid attention to what the doctor had said.

The Sister pulled a chair to the side of the bed and wrote on the clipboard she'd taken from the end of the bed. 'I'll do your obs now, okay? Then you can get a nice sleep before we bother you again.'

'Sister,' said Prudence, as the warmth of the opiate began its work, 'there was a young man in the Accident and Emergency ward with me ... very vocal; quite ... ill.'

'I can't discuss other patients, I'm sorry. I'll give you your night sedation now. Alright?'

'It's just ... thought he was the Galloway boy. His mother worked at the dry cleaners. A good friend...' Prudence drifted, but saw the Sister nod affirmation. 'Can't tell you anymore.'

Byron Galloway. The son of that poor woman. The one who had confided in her on that wintery day when torrential rain had emptied the dry-cleaning store of customers. The day the woman had disappeared, left her abusive husband. That was the talk anyway. She'd often wondered if she could have done more. Talked to the police? And say what? Jean Galloway hadn't been reported missing. Not by her own family. Adults were allowed to go where they pleased.

There was the shadow of a memory, filed succinctly at the back of her mind. A memory that had been stirred by the sight of Jean's son in dire straits. What was it? That darn sedative.

The pale face of Jean Galloway flitted through her mind as she tried to focus on the bouquet of white lilies Earl had brought her.

Jean Galloway sat in the chair by her bed. 'Is it time to go home yet, Prue?' Jean's blonde hair was longer and it shone so brightly that Prudence shut her eyes.

'You know your own hours, Jean. I don't have to tell you

when to go home.' Prudence was pleased to see Jean but those bright colours. Jean was dressed in aqua and gold. 'You're not in uniform, Jean.'

'Is it time to come home yet, Prue? I've waited so long.' Jean swung her hair. 'Home, Prue. Is it time?' Her voice grew softer. She wasn't as vibrant. The colours faded. Jean's face contorted. The room darkened. Jean screamed, 'find me, Prue, find me.'

'Mrs Wainwright, Mrs Wainwright.' A voice interrupted Jean's cries for help. Someone was shaking her shoulder gently, interfering with her conversation that was important. She pushed the hand away.

'I have to help a friend get home,' said Prudence. 'Or is it to get somewhere else … Why can't I remember?'

'It's all right, love. You're in the hospital.' A torch swung round the room, lighting up dull walls, a chair and an over-bed table. 'You're doing fine.'

'But my friend Jean was here. She…' Prudence pushed herself up onto her elbows.

'I doubt it, love. Everyone's trying to get out of this place.'

The night nurse cracked a wry laugh, then checked the IV, Prue's observations and straightened the bed. 'Just a dream, love. You've had quite a shock, but your blood vessels have stents now to help the flow. You're one of the lucky ones. I have your next meds.'

Stents, what the heck were stents? Why did nurses ramble on in lingo with that smug look as if they were completely understood? Lucky ones, lucky stents, sucky onety stenty,' Prudence repeated as she drifted back to who knows where…

Snooping

Bridget's relationship with her father's horsey friend Carol swung from indifference to annoyance.

When Bridget wandered into the kitchen early in the morning after Byron had been discharged she found Horsey Carol placing a box of fruit and veg on the bench. It was a generous size box and had lovely fresh produce.

Carol jumped and held a hand on her throat. 'Oh my Lord, I thought you'd be at school. You never miss a day.' She bit her lip. 'I mean, er ...' Her voice descended to a whisper.

'You're the one who brings stuff from the market?'

'Yes,' Carol leaned awkwardly against the bench eyeing the gap between Bridget and a possible exit.

'Why are you here? Why do you hang around Da?'

'Well, it's, I, er...'

Byron slouched into the room. 'Chill Bridgee, haven't you heard of good Samaritans.' He grabbed a lush apple, bit into it with a satisfying crunch, juice running down his chin. He grabbed two more, stuffing them into pyjama pockets.

'Don't take them all, Byron. I give some to Jessie.'

'Who's Jessie?

'The horse in our south paddock.'

'Oh well, sis, generosity comes full circle, that's Carol's horse.'

A slow smile crept over Carol's face as she glided sideways out of the room.

'Ah Bridgee, that filly is Carol's pride and joy. She agists two sections of our land and pays with this little lot, and a few other things that I can't recall this minute.'

'It's a wonder you can recall anything after your hospital stay. I'm surprised you're upright. They told me you were completely out of it. I was so worried.' Bridget wipe a pyjama sleeve across her sniffling nose.

'Ah sis, I was okay. Just having a nap.'

'Nap, my arse.' Bridget poked his chest and he crumpled in mock defeat. 'Leave the apples. I'll cook you some breakfast.'

'Yes, ma'am. I'll have some salty sausages if you please.'

Bridget groaned and set about preparing while Byron slumped in the closest kitchen chair.

'How'd you get home from hospital, Byron?'

'Carol.'

'Oh. That's odd.'

'Not as odd as me walking, collapsing by the roadside and being taken back to the ward.'

'You're honestly not bothered with that horsey woman pushing her way in? I don't get why she hangs around Da.'

'Yeah, well, I'll admit that's a mystery right there. But I don't care. It's a bonus having decent food and she keeps the old dude occupied. Keeps him off your case. She's clearly not after money.' Byron gave a croaky laugh and slapped his leg. 'So I say let's give horsey Carol her due. Never know when she might come in handy.'

'User!' Bridget flicked him with a teatowel.

Carol came-in-handy sooner than expected.

It wasn't the first time that Tom Galloway had suffered a fall, but it was certainly a superior effort. He broke his femur and that would require surgery and rehabilitation.

Byron had escaped the mad house again. He seemed to have an endless list of friends with spare rooms or comfortable couches.

Bridget had been at school when the accident happened. However, Carol had organised everything, even throwing a pair of pyjamas in a plastic bag with a toothbrush for him.

It was strange to come home from school with only a quick phone call from Horsey Carol. Thank goodness for the phone. Da would never have given her one. And she didn't want him to know she had one now. Could she trust Horsey Carol not to tell him?

Horsey Carol's offer to pick her up from school was an opportunity to test her out.

It was a nightmare drive. The short distance back to the house seemed like a marathon. Horsey Carol talked rapidly all the way, jiggled the gear stick as if she'd never driven a stick-shift before. She drove leaning forward, tapped the brakes on corners and hesitated at every turn, left or right.

'Er, thanks, um, Carol. For the fruit and stuff, for like everything, y'know. Um, here's the thing, Da doesn't know I have a phone. He, er, won't let me have one, so, I, um...'

'...he won't hear it from me, Bridget. You can trust me on that. I'll still come by with fruit and veg. Is there anything else you would like?'

Bridget's hopes rose then crashed. She was no good at asking for help. Staring at the floor, she mumbled.

'What was that dear? I can take you shopping if you like? There must be things you need. Personal, or ... um'

Bridget's head flung up. The few shops in walking distance didn't have the things she needed and she'd saved up her wages from working at the hair salon with Iris, the local hairdresser.

'Oh yes, there are,' Bridget said.

'How does MYER at the Colonnades sound?'

'Cool.'

'I'll drive the automatic next time. I hate driving my brother's wreck.'

Bridget giggled, quickly covering her mouth.

Carol's amusement was evident in her eyes.

After two days of rattling around the house alone Bridget phoned Jenna and Ebony. She could have gone to visit them. She could ride the bike Ebony's father had given her. It had been strange having things given to her. She'd objected but she'd been no match for the girls or Mr Harcourt who declared he never wanted to see the bloody thing again after it had kicked like a mule. It was now clogging up his garage and he'd be glad to see the back of it. He wasn't like his agile wife who was great on rollerblades and anything with wheels. He'd stick to a car, thank you very much.

The girls arrived with snacks and curiosity. Or at least Jenna did, but it didn't take long for her mood to catch on.

The lounge room had light streaming in and the lacquered furniture shone like new. All the faded tapestry cushions on the lounge chairs had been turned over. A vase of fresh flowers had replaced the ever-present over-filled ash tray on the rickety coffee table.

'Sheesh, wouldn't recognise the place. What happened, Bridge?' asked Jenna. 'There's so much light in here.'

'The occupational therapist came and did a risk assessment. She shifted everything around. I'm glad she did it because Da wouldn't let me touch a thing.'

'I wish the occupational therapist would do my room then. This is great.'

'She'd never be seen again if she went into your room Jenna,' said Ebony.

Halfway down the narrow hallway, Jenna paused at a dark door. 'What's this room?' Jenna sneezed at the dust as she entered the room. 'Clearly she didn't come in here.'

'Don't go in there. That's Da's private place.' Bridget ran to stop her.

The room had dark, dusty furniture, heavy curtains of an indiscriminate fabric, so old it was difficult to tell their original colour. The room had the musty smell of years of neglect.

'It's not much bigger than a cupboard. What's he keep in here? Ooh, we might find something about your mum,

Bridge.'

'Don't poke around Jenna, it's … oh, shit!' Bridget slumped into the nearest chair as Jenna started opening drawers and Ebony stared into a large wardrobe that dominated the small room.

'He keeps a lot of papers. I thought he'd have Jim Beam in the cupboards.' Ebony stared at a pile of folders. 'Gosh, this is pretty tidy. You sure this is your father's room?'

'Maybe he's never been in here for years.' Jenna opened another drawer. 'Ah, photographs. These will be interesting. Have you seen these before, Bridget?'

Bridget was hooked, but worried. 'I … no.'

'Don't worry,' said Jenna, we'll put everything back exactly as we found it. That's the first rule of a snoop, I mean private investigator. I've seen how Dad works.' Jenna placed the drawer on the floor and began to lift each photograph carefully, while rambling on to the other two how spies would leave small things out of place in someone's flat so that they'd be put off kilter without knowing why, just small shifts of ordinary things. This marvellous information didn't impress the other two who were fascinated by the photographs.

The three girls sat on the floor on a low pile carpet that had very little wear and tear. The photographs had been stored carefully. None were bent or wrinkled.

Bridget knew only a few of the people in the photographs.

'The names are written on the back,' she said, 'but that's not much help. These are probably cousins or relatives of Mum or Da, I wouldn't know. Never met half of them and they'd look different anyhow. Ethel, John, Tom, I guess that's Da's brothers and sister.'

'We'll put their names down and look them up,' Jenna took out a notebook. 'On Trove.'

Bridget found a beautiful photograph of her mother absorbed in painting. 'I wonder if Da would miss one if I took it,' she said, gently touching her mother's face.

'Take it. I reckon he wouldn't notice. This lot was at the bottom. We can always use our mobiles to take pics. That way nothing would be different and you'd have copies.' Jenna took out her smart phone, selected an app and enhanced a few of the ones Bridget had put aside.

'Who's this?' Ebony held up a photograph of a dark-haired woman pegging clothes on the line in one photo, leaning wistfully against a shed wall in another. 'It says "Shirl" on the back. How odd?'

Bridget took the photo and looked closely. 'I've never seen her. That's our back shed though.'

'Have you ever checked old newspapers?' Jenna clicked her phone, capturing the image. 'Ebony did that to find out about her mum.'

'I dunno how to do any of that investigating stuff. Never go to the library. And I just ... well, Da said...'

'...and he's never lied?' said Jenna, blowing dust off a photograph.

'Oh crap, you're right. I've just sat here all these years with Da's story in my head. Where would we start? Wait on, Mum worked for Mrs Wainwright. They talked. She might know something.'

'Then that's where we start,' said Jenna.

A red chesterfield

'He's a rare man,' said Mrs Wainwright, 'rare indeed.'

Jenna shrugged. Ebony stared. Bridget listened.

Bridget, Ebony and Jenna were seated on a red Chesterfield three-seater, that Jenna, who had mixed in the most opulent of places, realised would have cost more than their parents' cars.

They'd been admitted to the house by Willow. This in itself had been a shock.

Bridget was stunned into silence by the room. The house possessed the kind of elegance and styling she'd only seen in magazines. Apart from the corner where Earl Wainwright, Mayor and business owner, sat, surrounded by baby rugs, toys and nappies.

'A rare man,' repeated Prudence Wainwright.

The girls shared confused looks. Was Mrs Wainwright okay? What was she talking about?

Ebony leaned forward and took a breath.

Jenna sensing an error in tactics, pulled her back, earning a puzzled shake of the head from Ebony until she remembered her dreadful row with Mrs Wainwright at the school.

Ebony, on the other hand, viewed Jenna as universally blunt and not to be trusted on this venture. As it was, Mrs Wainwright was acting very differently to her normal self, which was apparently common for people after heart attacks—she'd overheard Emma.

Jenna objected to Ebony's facial expression and gave her a look that was supposed to be explanatory and also warning. On both accounts it fell short.

Ebony pointed at Earl Wainwright on the other side of the large room. Instead of his regal clanking Mayor's chain he had a plastic chain that was attached to a pacifier. He had the back end of the pacifier between his teeth and was gurgling to a dusty brown baby with a thatch of fiery red hair.

Bridget placed a hand on Mrs Wainwright's arm. 'It's very kind of you to have us here, Mrs Wainwright.' This had the desired effect of bringing Mrs Prudence Wainwright out of her reverie and cognizant of her surroundings, at least to a degree.

'Bridget, that's so lovely of you. What marvellous manners. Just like my Earl over there. Some are born with it, I say. My daughter Willow will get you some lemonade. Oh there she is.'

Willow placed a tray of cold drinks in frosted glasses in front of the girls and gave her mother a steaming cup. 'Tea for you, Mother. No more coffee.'

'Yes dear,' said Mrs Wainwright, accepting the tea.

'You girls okay?' asked Willow, establishing her role as caretaker.

The girls nodded.

Willow sat on the floor near Earl.

The girls drank quietly. This scene was not what they had expected. The News item had shown a chaotic scene outside the A&E where it was explained that the dark woman with the curly red hair was the secret love child of Mrs Prudence Wainwright and an unknown man. It appeared that Prudence's heart attack had taken second place to her new status as the latest cause of scandal for having a love child.

The news had set the town chattering.

Everyone expected that the secret daughter would quickly disappear, induced to do so by the stiff Prudence Wainwright and the sure-to-be-embarrassed, highly respected Mayor, Earl Wainwright. But the girls, given entrance to the grand house with its opulent velvet curtains and red chesterfield seating, were shocked not only by the clutter of baby gear, but by the signs of complete domesticity of the newly connected family.

Bridget reached for Prudence's cup when it began to clatter on the saucer. 'Are you sure it's alright for us to come, Mrs Wainwright?'

'Oh sure,' said Prudence as she leaned back in the chair and stared at one of the three chandeliers in the room. 'My Earl, who would ever think that a man could be so compassionate and forgiving.'

'Nothing to forgive, Prue dear,' he said, 'all before my time, lovey.'

Jenna and Ebony signalled to each other that perhaps it might be better to leave. Prudence Wainwright seemed in no position to conduct a useful conversation that might reveal anything about her last encounter with Jean Galloway at the time of her disappearance. Besides, it seemed that Bridget was doing a better job of the whole enterprise and if Mrs Wainwright became aware of the presence of Ebony and Jenna she might clam up. They sat back as far as they could in the red chesterfield.

'Your sweet mother,' Prudence said, seeking Bridget 'Mysterious thing that. I assumed that your father would see the police, put in a Missing Person's report, but the next thing I heard was that dreadful rumour that she had run off with a sales rep. Never, not Jean. Something not quite right about the whole thing. She didn't collect her last pay, and ...' Prudence rested her head back on the recliner.

Earl, watching carefully, rose to his feet, handing the baby to Willow, who left the room so swiftly with all the baby gear that one would wonder if she was ever there.

With one hand on his wife's shoulder, Earl told the girls that Prudence was tiring. They rose to leave with a chorus of apologies. However, Earl quietly requested that Bridget stay, for 'a little chat'.

Silently, Bridget sat on the edge of the settee.

Ebony and Jenna nodded, repeated more grovelling apologies and walked to the door Earl held open for them.

'I'll drop Bridget home,' Earl said.

Once the door was closed, Jenna said, 'Wow, no wonder people respect him. I thought he got things done by being bossy but he's so kind that you want to do whatever he says.'

'But why does he want to talk to Bridget?' Ebony asked, picking up her bike.

'We don't have to go. We could wait here.' Jenna sat on the steps.

'That would be rude, like spying.'

'Yeah, but that's what we're doing. Spying.'

On the other side of the door Earl Wainwright sat opposite Bridget, leaning with his elbows on his knees, hands folded loosely.

'Bridget, Prue and I have been talking about this. In the hospital she, well, she thought she saw your mother, the morphine of course, but it set her thinking and wondering. She couldn't let it rest, and that's one thing I love about her, it's better to get things off her chest. She always felt that your mother was a missing person. Prue approached the police when your mother first went missing.'

'Oh, I didn't know that.'

'A sergeant came to the house. He said they'd spoken to your father and your father said your mother didn't come home after work the night before she was due to go to work, the night before she went missing.'

'But she did, she did. She had plans for my birthday. She...' Bridget choked on a sob.

Prudence Wainwright was startled into speech. 'Yes, she did, she was excited about it, although a bit mysterious ... But I saw her the next morning, out of the front of the house waiting for a taxi. My driver waved. She did seem a bit ...' Prue's voice faded off.

Bridget wrung her hands. 'She was there that night. Although who'd believe me. I was only six. If it hadn't been my birthday the next day I probably wouldn't have remembered. And the next day, my birthday, she didn't come home. Da was supposed to be off, um, at some tractor show I think. Don't remember that bit.'

'What you remember is important, Bridget. It doesn't matter that you were six at the time. It must have been an incredibly hard time for you. I imagine that you were lost and afraid when your mum didn't come home.'

'Da said she ran off with a man.' Bridget's hair hung over her face.

'We don't think that's true. We don't know what happened, Bridget.'

Bridget's eyes met his.

'Earl?' Mrs Wainwright moaned and Earl rose and went to her. 'Now, dear, you must take it easy. I'll get Willow to get your medication while I say goodbye to Miss Galloway. Okay.'

There was a scurry as Willow attended to her mother as if she'd been around for years instead of weeks.

Earl put his hand lightly on Bridget's shoulder. 'Please feel that our home is open to you any time, Bridget.' He took a deep breath. 'You may be surprised at how easily I have accepted Willow and her baby. But life is short. And, well, every child is a blessing. 'I just want you to know that if you're confused or just want to talk, we're here.'

Bridget protested that she would ride her bike home, allowing Earl to rush back to his wife's side.

'Earl.' Prudence grabbed her husband's sleeve. 'I saw her. That morning. In her uniform. It was the day we had the new driver and leased that black town car.'

'That ugly thing. I sent it back.'

'Hush Earl.'

Earl squeezed her hand.

'I saw her, Earl. Waiting by the side of the road for a taxi.'

'I thought she caught the bus to work.'

'They were on strike that day. Do pay attention Earl.'

Earl zipped his lips dramatically.

'I sent the driver back to pick her up, Earl. But, I don't know the rest, or I've forgotten.'

Intrigued

Adam Price looked out the window of his 3rd storey office in Marion. He shouldn't be at work on the weekend. His secretary, Delia, would give him the rounds of the kitchen if she knew. She'd always been like a mother hen to him and became more so after Caroline's death. Was he avoiding home? That empty house. Perhaps he should move, but there would be nothing left of Caroline in his life.

This was one day he would write off—it was nearly lunchtime and he hadn't achieved anything productive. He was haunted by a different ghost today. The ghost of Leah Bond. Well, that's what she'd called herself. But he'd searched the web and come up with nothing. How could you only spend one day with a woman and find her returning to your thoughts with alarming regularity? It wasn't attraction, he told himself—it was simple curiosity. He was a lawyer and she was a puzzle. Like one of his crosswords, there were gaps. And there was nothing Adam Price hated more than missing pieces.

He'd thought he had her pegged a few times. Weird, reclusive, dressed like a cult member. Then when she'd been a bit tipsy and less inhibited, he'd seen another side; childlike warmth and humour.

It would have been a nice neat bundle if they hadn't been detoured to Melbourne. There would have been no loose ends. But when they landed he'd seen fear in her eyes. Not like the panic she experienced with the turbulence on the plane, but real fear. She'd looked over her shoulder most of the time.

Sometimes he was angry that they had met at all. He didn't need a vulnerable woman, and Leah was troubled. They should have simply shared a quick plane trip, but the unexpected detour to Melbourne had put paid to that. He should have stayed right away from her. That was what he intended when he strode towards the airport bus.

However, they'd ended up at the same hotel and she'd joined up with that married couple, the Burnsides; nice people. John, was not a bad chess player, and his wife was Brenda, the realtor. He knew that because he was holding her business card, and it was the reason he was hovering near the phone. It was a connection to Leah, and she was weighing on his mind.

It had been quite a jolt to walk off the plane straight into an agitated dark-haired man in a black suit. It had taken a moment to realise this was not the same man they'd seen in Melbourne, the one Leah had shrunk from, although the resemblance was uncanny. The man had approached Adam.

'Was this woman on the plane? I've asked everyone else on

the bloody plane. Someone must know. Have seen her.'

The man thrust a photograph of a fashionable blonde woman in Adam's direction. Adam didn't like to be caught off guard, so he took his time looking at the photo, while shaking his head. The woman was unfamiliar, at first. Thankfully, he took a moment longer because the woman was definitely Leah. A different Leah. *'I'm not myself'*, he remembered her saying. She'd mentioned a man's name and rambled on about perfection and some guy. Damn, why couldn't he remember the guy's name?

He played for time. 'Don't think so. Looks like a woman you would notice though,' he said. 'Can't be positive? Who is she? An escaped felon?' He smiled. 'Have you got another photo, um, Mr...?'

Adam waited.

'Never mind,' said the man. Snatching the photo he strode towards a thick set, dark-suited man whose furtive glances and dark glasses combined to make him appear ill at ease. His tie was loose and he was scowling. As the first man approached he stood straighter and dropped the impatient stance. The man who had spoken to Adam flicked the photo, waved his arms angrily. He opened his wallet and gave the second man a roll of bank notes. The roll was accepted with a deferential, brisk nod.

Adam Price stared blankly at the traffic below. Things were beginning to add up. Leah Bond was in some kind of trouble. He was sure of it.

Shuffling papers aimlessly on his desk, Adam reached for

his wallet and found Brenda Burnside's business card. He had tried to put the dilemma about Leah out of his mind, but it had refused to shift. It was 8 am. They were sure to be home. He dialled the home number, then cursed when the phone rang out.

Leah ignored the phone.

If anyone wanted Bren or John they could leave a message. They were the only two people in the world who didn't rely solely on mobiles.

If she didn't get a job soon she'd go mad. She was nearly ready to work at the local Fish & Chip shop, except she'd feel too exposed there. A lot of people came through there in a day. No, what she needed was a nice quite corner in an office.

Leah wandered into Bren's kitchen and waited for Bren and John's cat, Angus Almighty to favour her with his presence. She had become accustomed to the large cat and his aristocratic ways. Feeding him for John and Bren was something she enjoyed doing. Anything she could do to feel useful was a plus these days.

Angus appeared and accepted his gourmet dinner.

'Your mistress thinks I would make a good secretary, Angus.'

Angus looked up at her and blinked.

'I really want a job where there are no people,' she added. 'I guess that's asking too much. I should have done databases—then I could hide out in a dark corner with just a computer. Why didn't I do that, Angus?'

Angus tilted his head and meowed.

'Oh, did I forget your biscuit topping?' Leah picked up the bag with the small gourmet biscuits and sprinkled a few on Angus's meal. Instantly gratified, he purred and began to munch loudly.

Leah sat down and sighed. 'There's a woman coming to drop papers off, to interview me. I wish your mistress was home, Angus. I don't want to meet anyone. Maybe if I don't answer the door she'll leave the papers in the letterbox. Or ... I could go out ...'

If Angus approved of this endeavour, the slow flicking of his tail gave nothing away.

'I will.' Leah picked up her purse and the house keys and headed for the door. On opening the heavy timber door she realised there was a slight blonde woman standing on the doorstep holding a sheaf of papers. With her back to Leah, she appeared to be admiring the view. Leah considered a hasty retreat, but it was too late. The woman had heard the door opening and turned towards her with a radiant smile.

'Hello, you must be Leah,' the woman said, 'My name is Emma Harcourt. I'm here to help.'

Totally unprepared, Leah swallowed back tears. She turned to open the door for Emma. This gave Emma a clear view of the now faint bruising on Leah's neck. Emma had worked too long at the polyclinic not to recognise the signs of domestic abuse.

'James can't know I'm here...' said Leah, hiccupping. 'This paperwork won't...'

'We're not in the habit of contacting bastards!' Emma said.

Leah choked back a giggle. The normality of Emma's

reaction put her at ease. 'I guess I should start at the beginning,' she said.

'Good grief no! I'd rather you started at the end—the now. I can guess the beginning, Leah. Gentle country girl goes to the Big Smoke to make her mark, meets a handsome Prince Charming, feels loved for the first time, marries him. He turns into a wicked controlling ogre, smacks her around, then gives superior grovelling apologies before doing it all over again. How am I doing so far?'

Leah's mouth formed an O. 'Goodness. Have you met him?'

'No, just dozens of his relatives—Creepy, Sulky, Sneaky ...'

'Oh stop!' laughed Leah. 'Honestly, you're not what I thought of a community nurse. How do you do it? I can't believe you understand so well. Are you a social worker?'

'No, I'm the clinic nurse, friend of Bren and John. The social worker won't be this blunt.' Emma frowned. 'Where is this James?'

'Sydney.'

'Well, that's a bit of good news. He will look for you though, if I'm not mistaken. Men like that usually do.' said Emma. 'I'll get a pot of tea, and you can tell me all about it. Have you left for good? It's no use setting things up otherwise, you know.'

'Yes, Oh yes.' Leah sunk into the soft luxury of the sofa.

The solemn grandfather clocked ticked a slow rhythm as Emma gathered the teapot and began the simple reassuring motions of preparing tea. Her silence did more to motivate Leah to share her story than all the probing questions and penetrating stares of her staff, friends and her sister.

While the steamy mist of Bergamot tantalised the air, Leah cradled her dainty teacup and opened her heart and her life to the nurse, sparing little in the telling. Emma showed no shock or surprise and didn't interrupt with questions until Leah leant back in the chair, exhausted.

'What made you choose Noarlunga? Was it Bren? She's a darling. But small towns aren't necessarily the best places for anonymity, sweet, if that's what you need right now. You'll have to face James one day, you know, but not alone. Only in court. Then, you'll never have to lay eyes on him again. You don't have custody issues.'

Leah sighed.

'I'm sorry, I know you feel it's too much too soon.' Emma patted Leah's knee. 'Tell me what you want to happen now.'

'I know I'll have to face James, but not yet. I'd like a job. Out of the limelight.'

Emma nodded. 'What skills do you have?

'I waitressed a bit, but that's no good. Um, I did mail send-outs to earn money at Uni.'

'There's a job going in the council offices. I'll see what I can do,' said Emma. She paused. Leah was vulnerable, she needed to tread softly. 'And family?'

Leah groaned. 'I have a sister, Stephanie, but she's as taken in with James as everyone else.'

'She'll see. In time.'

'I don't know. He's very good.'

'Yes, controlling men are extremely skilled. They have to be charming and personable, but sooner or later the wheels come off. I'm just glad you're safe. Tomorrow is another day. I'll set you up with a good counsellor.'

   'A what?'

   'You'll like him.'

   'But a shrink?'

   'They'll phone you with an appointment.'

The shrink

Dr Kent's waiting room was straight out of a lifestyle magazine, just as Emma had said when she recommended the man. The receptionist took her details and told her that because this was her first appointment the session would last an hour and a half.

'Oh,' said Leah.

'Doctor will call you shortly.' The receptionist smiled reassuringly.

The doctor called Leah just as she'd taken a seat opposite the fish tank. She was escorted to a spacious corner office where she sat opposite a large older man, who maintained eye contact while writing brief notes. Leah relaxed. Relaying the facts had less sting than she'd imagined.

She was unprepared for his next question.

'When did it become okay for James to abuse you?'

Leah gasped. All her ideas of being in therapy as a soothing ramble through a lifetime of misaligned hopes that arrived with gift-wrapped answers were dashed in that instant. She thought counsellors were supposed to listen, not interrogate.

'What are you thinking right now, Leah?'

Leah clamped her jaw tightly and focused on the rolling surf just visible through the window. It was a strange window; even though it faced the best view in town, it was a long panoramic slice rather than taking advantage of the beauty of the coastline. 'Take your time if you need to,' said the calm, fatherly man in front of her. Calm. A state of being she'd forgotten about. Calm. It was a pause between storms for her. But this man exuded it. How had he managed to be granted such a liberal dose of what she lacked? Would she ever know calm again?

Leah remembered the sense of panic when she walked in and Dr Kent had shut the door behind them. In that moment she'd realised she hadn't been alone in a room with a man since James. Although there was no rational reason, fear gripped her. Fleetingly she thought of Peter Pan and how he had lost his shadow. Why couldn't she lose the shadow of James? Of fear?

'I don't know what I'm supposed to say,' she said finally.

'You don't trust yourself enough to share?' he asked quietly.

Leah flushed.

'I don't trust this ... you, it's not about trusting myself. I don't...'

'So who have you trusted? Tell me about the last person you trusted.'

'Well you can't ... really trust anyone but yourself. It's ...'

'So you only trust yourself. How's that working for you?'

'It's ... oh God ... you're confusing me.'

'This isn't going the way you thought, is it?' he said, 'You've been thinking that James and his abuse is the only area of your life that's out of whack and if you could only put enough distance between the two of you, then your life could return to normal.'

Leah shook her head vehemently—then burst into tears. 'Yes. Yes, that's what I think. I didn't ask, I didn't choose ...'

'But you did.'

Leah's shocked eyes flew upwards, but she saw only gentle concern in the face of the man. He would have been about her father's age. She had no reason for it, but she felt a sudden rush of anger towards this man. In all her time with James she hadn't returned anger for abuse. Not once. But here, with a stranger, a confronting stranger, she felt a tight band of rage crush her chest. For a brief moment it was so strong she thought she might faint.

'I didn't choose abuse, I didn't choose bruising. I didn't choose fists. I didn't choose to be the object of his rage. I didn't choose *this* -' Leah pulled back her sleeve and showed Dr Kent the scar across her wrist. 'This ... see this, he did this. He slashed my wrist, then called an ambulance. It was deliberate, planned; like some sick game. Who plays those kinds of games? Who harms the one they've promised to love and protect? That's what I said yes to ... *not this.*' Leah slumped in the chair, deflated. She hadn't intended to say any of this, she'd never revealed the story of her injury. And still she was holding her arm out for him to see. The arm she had protected from view. She let her arm slump onto her lap, but didn't bother to drag her sleeve to cover it as she had a thousand times before.

'It took a lot of courage to tell me that, to show me. I can't help but think that this is perhaps the first time you've been honest and real about that terrible episode and I want to thank you for trusting me with it.'

'I don't know why I'm here,' said Leah.

'You chose to come.'

Leah groaned. There was that word again.

'You may feel pressured, but you chose to walk through that door. Somewhere within you is the question of why. Why did this happen to you? And it will shock you to learn that it's not about who James is, but who you are, what you allowed.'

'I don't understand any of this ... I ...'

'I will ask you one question, and then I'll give you some homework. Okay?'

'Okay.'

'If James had asked you to help him rob a bank, would you have gone along with it?'

'Of course not! He would never have changed my values. My...'

'But you let him rob you, and those you love; again and again. It was you he didn't value. Because you didn't value yourself. You had boundaries about violent crime against banks, but not about you, about Leah. There was a reason for that and I will tell you why you're here. To take a long road, a narrow path back to loving yourself. It will involve being real in a way you've never been before. It will confront and confuse you. It will stretch everything you know. Will you trust me to walk that road with you?'

Leah wiped a single tear. 'Yes. I will.' She was gripped with equal parts of terror and hope. Terror—she knew well, but hope—that was something so new and so distant it seemed more frightening than the familiarity of the terror she knew so intimately. But, what if it were possible? To hope? To believe in living and being more?

'What's my homework?' she asked.

'Buy a journal, write how you felt about being here today and bring it next time you see me. Write without thinking, planning or wondering why—can you do that?'

'It won't be clever or careful or even make sense.'

'That's okay. That's perfect.'

Leah left the room like a deflated balloon. She sorted payment with the receptionist mechanically before taking the stairs to the ground floor. Gazing at her watch, she felt a profound sense of relief that she had half an hour before seeing Emma. Then she'd tell her counselling just wasn't for her, thanks anyway, it wasn't her cup of tea. She couldn't see it achieving anything. The cure was worse than the disease. It was different for Bridget, different altogether.

She bumped into a woman with a pram who gave her a questioning look. There, that's what comes of poking around in Pandora's Box, from opening up your feelings. She was so churned up she couldn't see straight.

The beach was dotted with post-tourist crowds. A walk would clear her head. Help her regain her fragile equilibrium. Wandering without a sense of purpose, other than to escape the thoughts that the last hour had brought to life, she dragged her feet in the edges of the white froth of the retreating surf. The voices of laughing children tantalising the remnants of summer days faded. Even the noise of the traffic receded. The breeze ruffled her hair into her eyes, but she resisted the urge to undo the tight coil held by the barrette.

She didn't want to go back to Dr Kent. He'd opened wounds, deep nasty wounds that brought the whole problem to her feet. Instead of seeing a light at the end of the tunnel, all she'd felt was a greater sense of panic than before.

An angry voice intruded. A woman's shrill voice. A man's begging reply. Leah froze. The air had chilled. She was nearly at the headland, much farther than she had intended. Without looking up she ran. Those angry voices had triggered a panic attack.

She ran the full length of the beach, arriving white faced at the café where Emma was waiting.

'It was awful, but I can't run forever. I need this. I'll go back.'

Salon

Laying on her back watching the play of the shadows created by the trees outside her window in the pale moonlight, Leah thought about the length of her days, the boredom. Missing her passion for design.

When had she lost herself? Maybe it wasn't too late. Having Bren as a friend, finding Emma, had made her realise how little self-esteem she possessed after her years with James. When she'd fled, she thought she would be happy to embrace anonymity forever, but she had missed so much. She wanted to be part of things again. Everywhere there seemed to be happy couples, mothers or fathers with children, woman having coffee with friends or shopping together.

Work hadn't filled the lonely hours. She'd chosen exile, but once embarked on it she was lost about how to step out and still be safe. Now, she had a chance to change things. She loved the fashion industry and longed to make classic business wear and feminine casual clothing. She'd been drawing ideas in the flat at Bren and John's. It was a start. She would only stay a short time with them. She didn't want to live in fear anymore.

She stole a glance at the mirror beside the bed. Looking back at her was a faded woman. A woman with a shrunken life. Leah could have smashed the mirror. Her anger surprised her. Why, not long ago she had been a celebrated fashion designer.

How had she let James take that from her?

No, she had let it go, surrendered it. Chosen, like Dr Kent said. She, Leah, had become the dowdy person looking back in the mirror, and she didn't like what she saw.

She took out her journal. Her sessions with Dr Kent had become a regular part of her life, and he was right, it was a long road, both confronting and confusing. She was beginning to make connections with her past. At times she felt that the whole history of her life had been a myth that needed to be rewritten. However, she was beginning to understand her part, and herself. Maybe self-love was close behind. She looked at the last entry. It was titled 'Horizon' and only the words 'I have one' were scrawled underneath. Change was seeping into her life, so gradually that it was indefinable.

A sudden thought both elated and terrified her. A makeover. Did she dare? James didn't matter anymore. Hiding didn't matter anymore. Her inner self was beginning to feel the stretch of renewal. Why not the outside? She would do it. Starting with her feral hair.

'Well, wonders never cease,' said Iris, as she sipped her coffee and watched Bridget sweep the salon meticulously. 'I just made an appointment for that new woman. Fancy that, her wanting a change.'

Bridget looked up and gave a wan smile. 'She's probably been suppressed all her life,' she said philosophically. 'By her father, most likely,' she added, clutching the broom tighter.

'That would explain a lot,' said Iris, surprised by Bridget's remark. She relished the small confidences the girl occasionally allowed her.

This sentence was the most that Bridget had said in the time she had been helping at the salon. She came in an hour after school each day as well as Saturday mornings when the rush and bustle left little time for conversation.

At first, Iris had wondered how Bridget would cope with the noisy weekend crowd. However, Bridget had quickly adapted, bringing coffees, washing hair. All done quietly and efficiently.

It seemed the salon had become part of the social hub of Blue Bay Road on Saturday mornings, along with the coffee shop opposite. Behind the coffee shop was an outdoor dining area that sat on the beach. Colourful umbrellas in burnt reds and aqua flapped on windy days and diners could watch the surfers and throw screeching sea gulls scraps of food.

Several months had passed since Iris had noticed Bridget's longing stares into the salon from across the road. It was hard to miss the defeatism of the troubled girl. It hadn't escaped Iris' notice that Bridget always wore long sleeves and clutched at her wrists when she was anxious. Her brother, Byron, had quite a reputation for partying and drug use. Iris only hoped that Bridget hadn't followed his lead.

Knowing that Bridget would run a mile at any obvious

overture of friendship, Iris had waited until a particularly busy afternoon and beckoned to Bridget through the open salon door.

'Sweetie, are you doing anything right now?'

Iris held her breath. Bridget seemed poised to run.

'Could you possibly spare a bit of time to help me, just with clearing up? Jules, my assistant, had to go and pick her son up from pre-school.'

Bridget hesitated, like a fragile bird but Iris' softly pleading voice drew her closer. So often an object of pity or disdain it was refreshing to have someone react to her normally. She knew that most people thought she was seeking attention with her dark clothes and morbid air when the truth was that all she wanted was to fade into the background and not be noticed at all.

'I pay $20 an hour,' said Iris, sensing victory. Keeping her voice businesslike she waved her hand nonchalantly. 'There'll be other times I need help; if you're interested, that is.'

Bridget nodded mutely and came inside. While her demeanour screamed she would rather be anywhere on earth she listened carefully and followed Iris' instructions to the letter, uttering a muttered 'thank you' when Iris thrust a $20 note in her hand an hour later. There had been little conversation and Bridget had run out of the door as if the building was on fire. Iris kicked herself for not breaching the subject of the girl returning.

She was relieved a few days later when she spied Bridget hovering across the street in front of the coffee shop. Giving her a cheery wave Iris beckoned the girl over, unwilling to let another chance slip by. 'Bridget, I was hoping to see you. I wanted to ask if you could come in semi-permanently. Jules would like to leave earlier in the day so that she doesn't have to get a child minder for Ben after pre-school. Would you be interested? I was very pleased with your work.'

Bridget's eyes lit up. She flashed a brief but dazzling smile. 'I'd really like that,' she said. 'Oh, and thank you. Just tell me when. You won't be disappointed.'

Iris smiled as she watched Bridget work. The teen had been true to her word. She was a natural. The time would come when she could envisage offering the girl an apprenticeship. Of course, she'd have to work on that hair of hers. She'd been afraid to bring it up, hoping Bridget would come to her.

It was Bridget's artwork that surprised her the most. She'd seen the girl sketching and asked if she wanted to try to work on a hairstyle poster. The result was a slick, edgy image of a red-haired model.

Glad her intuition had paid off, Iris turned her attention to the new woman. 'What's your name, honey?' she asked. Now this is a rescue if ever I saw one, she thought, that hair. I don't know what she's done with it. Or not done.

'Leah, Leah Bond. My hair's a disaster. I'd like to go back to my natural colour. Grow it out. I wore it blonde for years but I ... well ... maybe a cut?'

'I can understand why you want to have your natural colour back. This regrowth is a lovely chocolate brown. It's a good ten centimetres now. If you'd like a cut you'd be rid of the dye. I can give you a treatment if you like. Then we'll shape.'

'Oh thank you. I'd love that.'

Sitting straight-backed and stiff Leah was a picture of tension while waiting for the treatment to work. She stole a look at Bridget and saw only empathy. And something else, she could have sworn she'd seen the girl before. Realisation dawned.

This was the girl from the shack. So she wasn't the only one hiding. Her heart lurched out to the girl, and inwardly she determined to do find out more.

When Bridget started sweeping near her, Leah murmured, 'um, do you remember me?'

Bridget looked up from her work, tilted her head, then nodded. 'The cemetery shack.'

Leah merely put a finger to her lips. 'That poster, is it one of yours? It's amazing.'

Bridget smiled. 'How did you…?'

'I saw the pastels in your backpack. You're very good. Do you do Art at school?'

'Yeah. But I'd better get back to … you know. Unless you want another coffee.'

'I'm good thanks. Um, right.'

Bridget returned to the soothing rhythm of her sweeping as she gathered the hair into the corner. She lost herself in the task and wondered at how the different strands of cut hair blended as she swept them. People who had never met now had their hair all tangled together. For a moment she allowed herself to admire the pattern at her feet. She would remember it for her sketch book later.

Iris returned to wash and cut Leah's hair after she'd taken payment from the previous client. With just Leah and Bridget in the salon, conversation died. There weren't many customers mid-week. Iris snipped and styled. At the end, Leah had a head of shiny curls.

'Wow,' said Leah. 'I've dyed and straightened my hair for so long just to please ... you know, but now I feel like myself.'

Standing nearby, Bridget couldn't help but be surprised. She'd worked at the salon for months but hadn't been this impressed with a transformation. 'That looks wonderful,' she said. It's nothing like the "you" that walked in.'

Maybe now I can talk you into a change, hey Bridget?' Iris stroked Bridget's hair, surprised the girl allowed this intimacy.

'That's nice. My mother used to ... I'd better go.'

Bridget left in time for an unseasonal downpour. Cursing the weather, she jumped when a car stopped beside her. With the window slowly gliding down she realised it was Leah, who began a rambling, nervous conversation.

'I know the rain is probably um ... would you like a ride home? It's bucketing down. And I could do with some company. Oh dear, I'm getting this all wrong aren't I, but I feel that I know you, Bridget.'

Bridget tensed, then sighed. 'Why not?' She shrugged, then opened the door listlessly and slid into the passenger seat.

Ever since the time in the cemetery shack Leah had wondered about the girl.

'Where do you live ...? Uh ... sorry ... where would you like me to take you?' asked Leah.

'Home, I s'pose,' said Bridget, struggling to click the

seatbelt.

'You don't sound sure. Are you hungry? I'm starving. How do you feel about us getting a bite? Maccas even?'

Bridget pulled a twenty dollar note from her pocket. 'Why the hell not. If Da finds my money he'll just take it anyway. What about the burger joint on the beach. I've enough for that.'

Leah smiled. She could have offered to pay but she didn't want to take any dignity from Bridget.

'So,' Bridget said, after she'd wolfed down half the burger. 'What's your deal? Running from an ex? Sorry if I'm prying but you look over your shoulder a lot and ... you know, you're kinda nervous, um Ms...'

Leah laughed. 'Just call me Leah. There's no use hiding anything from you, is there. Yeah, I left my ex-husband. He's ...'

'A bastard?'

'Yes. And he has bastard friends who he pays to keep his life in order. And right now I'm No.1 on that list. And now you, is there a reason you visit cemeteries in the middle of the night, other than for artistic purposes?'

'It's quiet there, and my father has usually passed out for the night. He has ... is ...'

'A bastard.'

'Yeah. How'd you get away then, um, Leah?'

'It all seems like a Mission Impossible movie now. A false name, a bad wig, new bank accounts and, most importantly, a neighbour who saw what was going on and shocked me out of the cycle and helped me get away on a flight.'

'Jeez, haven't got any of that.'

'I can give you a bad wig. But honestly, Bridget, someone cares,' whispered Leah. 'I care.'

Bridget angrily brushed at silent tears that slid down her face. 'Whatever.'

'Honestly, no-one should live like that. Let me help you find a way. To be safe.'

Bridget hesitated with her hand on the door. 'You're doing the most godawful, boring job on earth because you're hiding when you're so talented. You can't even face your own shit. How can you help me?' She wiped a sleeve across her eyes. 'There's no way out for me. It's different for me. I'm a kid. I gotta go.' She left with a quick, 'whatever. See ya. Thanks though.'

Bridget slammed the car door and ran into the downpour, holding her backpack awkwardly over her head.

Leah watched her leave, the backpack bouncing up and own. She felt terrible. She'd wrecked everything.

Catwalk

Stephanie Bond would never forget the night of Leah's fashion show. She'd overcome her nerves and opened the event with a few words. It wasn't as bad as she thought, she'd actually enjoyed it. Then she'd wandered down a side hallway. She wasn't supposed to be backstage. She didn't *want* to be backstage. The place was a maze of curtained areas, rushing assistants, half-dressed models, the cacophony of various appliances, the dull thud of the catwalk music, and chattering. Realising she was lost, Stephanie hesitated at the doorway to a room with mirrors lining the wall. She was about to enter when she heard a strident voice.

'Show me, child!' said a woman with red hair piled up like a bird's nest.

Stephanie stayed out of sight. She saw the woman pull on the young model's arm. Stephanie expected to see needle tracks or ... she didn't know what, she knew nothing of the modelling world. There was talk that drugs were rife. Nothing prepared her for the extensive bruising on the teen's arms.

Purple, blue and yellow marks glowed on both arms from shoulder to wrist.

The woman shrieked and covered her mouth.

'Can't you cover them up, Monique?' wailed the girl.

'Oh Liandra honey, I'm a maestro, not a magician.' Monique sighed, torn between anger and pity. 'This is the *Summer* collection sweetie. There are only a few beach caftans that would do the job, and they are the showstoppers. You've seen them; gorgeous butterfly silks, tigers and jungle prints. The bright colours are supposed to be in the garments, not your arms ... More importantly, what kind of lowlife did this to you?'

'Can't you use makeup? I've seen the television ads. There's miracle stuff out there. I just *can't* lose this opportunity; not after what I've been through. He'd never forgive me. I begged for this chance. This is my first big break. You could do it, Monique ... *please!* Can't you use that new stuff that covers tattoos?'

'Honey, I don't have enough makeup in my whole studio for these arms. What the hell happened to you?' But the girl was hiccupping, holding back a maelstrom of tears.

Monique crossed her arms. She didn't know anything about this new girl with the Bambi eyes and long legs other than her name. Usually she had to enhance the girl's faces, but this fragile child was near perfection. And there was something so heartrendingly innocent about her.

'Sophia!' she called over her shoulder.

'Oh, no! Don't tell anyone else,' moaned the elfin child.

'Too late for that, honey.' Monique ushered in Sophia, who

had a mouthful of pins.

'Oh my Lord, give me strength,' said Sophia, taking the pins out of her mouth slowly. 'Not again.'

'What do you mean, not again?' barked Monique, her head turning quickly to pierce Sophia with huge green eyes.

Sophia frowned and put the pins on the makeup bench. 'It's no use to be covering things up now. I'm done with this shady bus'ness. Keeping lids on things that's better in the open. Why in my country ... bah ... a man is a man. Big families we have, and if this thing happen to one of our women; always there is a brother to sort out the coward. Poor Miss Leah, she have no one, and always with bruises. I thought it would be the end of this bruise nonsense with her gone, but no. He has had his hands on others too, this child, Liandra. I'm gonna quit. I do this for Miss Leah for years. Promise not to tell, but she's gone now, godspeed to her, no point hiding anymore the truth about that sorry sonofabitch.' Sophia made the motion of spitting on the ground. 'Miss Stephanie soon will untwist that sad tale, she's a smart woman, that one. Better a man should do it, but Miss Stephanie will do it all right.'

'What are you talking about, Sophia?' asked Monique.

'Do you see nothing, Monique? All day you are looking at faces, into the eyes of women and you see nothing? You must know ... how can you mistake this? Mr James—he hits ... hits women. Why do you think Miss Leah she leaves—*for holiday in Bahamas?* No! Never would she let her girls down. Last time I see Miss Leah she had verrry bad bruises. This time on her neck. Usually he's too smart for that. Of course, he gets worse, a cut on her wrist I saw, ah yes, you can gasp *now!* That is the way these things go. First the flowers, too much flowers, always too much, then—bam! Do not talk of these men to me. Bah!'

'Sophia, please. We have to help this girl.'

'Ah, yes, of course, the bella Liandra. Did that rat "make the sweet love" to you too, eh? All right, all right ... I will help.' Sophia quickly left the room.

'Don't worry, honey. Sophia will think of something. But this must never happen again. We will see to it. Miss Stephanie won't stand for it.' Monique's brow furrowed.

Liandra snapped. 'Rubbish. She won't care. She has her head in the accounts all the time. If she couldn't see what was happening to her own sister, why would she believe me? No, you must say nothing. After tonight, if I'm lucky I'll get other work. Maybe over in Melbourne, or New York. If you tell her, I'll deny it. You hear me!' Liandra was shaking, her eyes fierce and determined.

Sophia returned with full-length skin-coloured gloves.

Stephanie slipped away.

Throughout that endless evening the pale face of Liandra haunted her, sometimes interposed with Leah's sad face. However, the shocking realisation that the girl was right, she would not have believed James capable of violence and would have stood behind him. That was what pierced her soul. She hadn't seen, hadn't known—hadn't wanted to know. The thought sickened her. She'd been as much in James's thrall as the simpering models surrounding him. Her own sister hadn't been able to confide in her.

And now she didn't have a clue where Leah was.

Liandra

Leah clutched the shiny plastic bag with the hair care products. She hadn't been able to resist the temptation of buying the shampoo and conditioner Iris had used. And just for good measure she'd purchased a pot of Moroccan oil treatment.

Iris was certainly a miracle worker. Leah's heart had thudded with worry throughout the snipping and drying. It wasn't until she saw her new glossy short hair that she sighed with relief. She looked wonderful.

She couldn't believe how Iris had managed to recapture the essence of the woman she'd once been. Just walking down the street with her hair free from its tight coil gave her a sense of freedom that sparked a forgotten memory of being totally herself. It was also a sobering reminder of how much of her self she had given away in exchange for a peaceful life with James.

Leah wasn't ready to go home. Bren would still be at work, but there was no reason she couldn't stop for a coffee by herself. She'd better get used to doing things on her own. Going back to isolation would be so easy, but she had lost enough.

Realising that she had never walked the entire length of the street, she began at the beach end and wandered up the street on the opposite side of the road to the salon. There was a restlessness that she couldn't name so she just went with the flow.

There were the usual tourist shops and take away venues that she had glimpsed, but then she caught sight of a boutique. It was slightly dated compared to the beach shops, but Leah saw a few lovely pieces of jewellery. Something there would suit Bren.

Yvonne Pettiford heard the front bell of her shop tinkle lightly. Sighing deeply she put her coffee cup in the sink and went from the storage area into the shopfront. A woman was browsing the Perspex jewellery cases, touching several pieces reverently. The woman was obviously lost in thought. Instincts honed over years of being a people-person made Yvonne slip quietly behind the counter, where she pretended to sort some lay-by dockets. She was proud of the quality of her garments and accessories and it was a real pleasure to see them enjoyed by a customer.

The woman turned and gave Yvonne a brief detached smile and Yvonne felt a shiver of recognition. 'Let me know if you need any help, dear. Is there anything particular you're looking for?' she asked.

'You have such gorgeous things, I thought I would buy a gift for a friend. She doesn't get much in the way of pampering. Thinks of others, you know the type. I owe her so much since

I arrived here. I want to think of a way to thank her.'

Yvonne continued to watch Leah from the corner of her eye as Leah admired the scarf rack. Yvonne knew so much more about the woman in front of her than Leah could ever guess. She struggled to open up the conversation that she wanted to have, this wasn't about her. It was for her beloved niece, Liandra. She finally blurted out, 'I know you. You're Leah Antoine, the fashion designer.'

'No!' Leah's head swung around swiftly and the scarf she was touching fell to the floor.

'Excuse me!' Leah began to back away towards the door.

'Oh please. I didn't mean to worry you. You have nothing to fear from me. Honestly.'

'I'm sorry. My situation is, er ... murky. Oh dear, I'm messing this up. Let me start again. Yvonne, I imagine you mentioned knowing me for a reason.' She looked around to see if any other customers were in the shop. It was empty.

'Please. Let me put the CLOSED sign up and put the kettle on,' said Yvonne.

'Why ever not! Goodness knows what shocking thing I'll say next.'

'I'm counting on it, dear.'

Perched on two plastic chairs with steaming cappuccinos the women sat opposite each other.

'I've had so much running around in my head and I need your help.' Yvonne said.

'That's fine. If you had suggested it a week ago I would have been on the next plane out.'

'I have a niece. Liandra, she's a model. She just did some work for your Summer Collection.'

'I wasn't at the showing for the Summer Collection.'

'I know.'

'My niece was assaulted ... your husband. A few times ... many. I don't believe she was the only one ...'

'James ... oh no! Oh God.' Leah's hands began to tremble and. 'Oh God, for so long you think you're the only one. That it's something you've done. How old is she, Liandra?'

Yvonne reached out and steadied the coffee cup .'Seventeen.'

'She has to go to the police. Oh, that's fine coming from me isn't it! I'm a great example.'

'She won't. She's a sensitive girl and she just wanted to put it behind her. She thought that by keeping quiet, she'd keep her work, but it hasn't worked out that way. She's lost a promising modelling contract. It seems more than a coincidence. And she's a nervous wreck, losing weight. I hate to mention it to you. I wouldn't have if you hadn't walked in here today ...'

'I'm glad I did. I'm sure I can help. Give me your niece's details and the agency. I'll make a few phone calls. I'll write my phone number down for you as well, in case. I go by my maiden name now. Leah Bond. But all this is between you and me. Right?'

'Oh, you are a dear. I wish I'd seen you sooner. You can't believe how worried I've been.'

'Sooner probably wouldn't have done any good. I wouldn't have been much good to you then. Liandra isn't the only one ...' Leah turned her wrist over 'to have something to fear from my husband.'

'Oh, you poor pet. Oh dear, I didn't mean to add to your woes.'

'You haven't, Yvonne. Trust me on that.'

Leah woke up with a plan. Bridget was right, how could she help anyone when she couldn't move forward herself? Bridget had awoken something in her, she reminded Leah of herself at that age. Wanting to be invisible, hiding a talent. Being so low in self-esteem had made her the perfect girl to be taken in by the smooth charms of James Antoine, man of the world. She remembered being so in love that she felt giddy and so fabulous to have such an urbane man take an interest in her. She had depended on him for her sense of herself instead of valuing herself and setting the bar. She'd fallen prey to his words. God forbid that Bridget would fall prey to a similar fate.

First, she would visit Yvonne Pettiford and let her know that her niece, Liandra could expect a phone call about her modelling contact. The thought of making a difference in someone else's life was an unexpectedly buoyant feeling. For so long she had been the victim in her own life that it was almost euphoric to be the hero for someone else. Someone who had survived what she had, someone just like her. Just like Bridget. Shadow girls.

That led her to a second inspiration. While she was at Yvonne's boutique she would do some serious shopping, some kickass extravagant girly shopping. She'd seen a fabulous halter neck dress in polished cotton with orange flowers and a skirt that flared elegantly. She'd had only lightly fingered the soft, shimmering fabric, but she knew it would suit her. It had been a long time since she had dared to see herself in something that bright and full of life, something that accentuated the curves that had reappeared now that she was eating like a normal person, and not someone trying to keep the interest of a straying husband who worshipped skinny.

She hoped one day that she'd be able to see Bridget in something other than black jeans and hoodie. She bought a denim jacket that would fit Bridget.

A summer jacket was added to her purchases. It would reveal the scar in her wrist. But there was a solution to that, a chunky bracelet would do just as well as the long sleeves she usually wore. Besides, she'd decided that she wasn't hiding anymore.

And it was time to move out of Bren and John's bedsit.

Bren helped Leah find a high-fenced, two-bedder cottage with a studio, a sunroom and a heavily shrubbed private back yard. Leah bought furniture, décor and kitchen equipment, surprised at how different her choices were from the house she'd shared with James. The cottage wasn't far from the Harcourts: Emma, Brady and Ebony, all of whom turned up along with Jack and Jenna to help with the move. Bren and John kept the sandwiches coming. It didn't take long.

Someone cares

As Da paced the kitchen, working himself up for a tirade or a beating, Bridget remembered Leah's eyes, full of concern. *Someone cares. Someone cares.* A hoarse whisper escaped her pale lips.

A hand was on the doorknob. Silence. Retreat. Thank God.

Her hand gripped the knife until her fingers cramped. Throwing it across the room she began to rock back and forth, sobbing.

She'd seen the change in Leah, she'd put weight on, new clothes, and smiles. At the salon she wasn't one of those toffy women who kept their heads in their magazines and expected a continuous supply of coffee, or wine, or both.

Staring at the rivulets of rain as they streamed down the window, Bridget remembered Leah's words.

The next time Leah was at the salon, Bridget approached shyly.

'I, I wouldn't mind a lift, if you're going my way, or … if …'

'Sure thing. Climb aboard,' said Leah.

'Oh, I'm sorry,' said Bridget suddenly aware of the silent tears sliding down her face. 'I'm sorry. I was so rude the other day.'

'Don't be,' said Leah, 'believe it or not, I know what it's like to fear someone, someone close.'

Bridget threw Leah a terrified glance. So this was what it was like to feel exposed, naked. She wrenched at the car door.

'Bridget, you're not alone. You don't ever have to be. Don't decide now. Come home with me. I have a place now. High fences. Security cameras. A place your father doesn't know about. We'll figure something out.'

'Well, here goes nothing,' Bridget said. Maybe if the pain could ease from Leah's eyes, something could work for her. Leah might bring some peace to her. She had certainly found it for herself. Anyway it was only one meal, one evening.

Bridget had seen the scar on her wrist, and felt at that moment that they shared something, perhaps not the same thing, but something.

'Okay,' she said, in such a tiny voice Leah had to lean towards her to catch it.

Spurring the car into action Leah did a U turn. Turning to Bridget, she smiled.

Bridget lowered her eyes. *Someone cares.*

Nightclub

'Wow.' Bridget had never seen an array of makeup like the collection spread before her at Jenna's. 'I'm a bit dizzy with this lot.'

'You don't get out enough,' said Jenna, expertly applying primer to her face.

'Do me!' Emma sat on the bed.

'Yeah, yeah. When I'm finished.' Jenna brushed Ebony's eager hand away from the makeup.

'I just want to try...'

'Wait.'

'It looks like an artist's palette,' said Bridget, her fingers itching.

'It is really,' said Jenna, slightly excited about being the only expert in the room, even though all of the girls had their own stash. 'I'll do both of you. I've a few tricks from hanging around Mum at work.'

'As long as we don't look like pantomime characters.'

Jenna shoved Ebony for that impertinence.

While the radio played *Dancing Feet*, Jenna worked her magic. As she brushed, massaged and applied foundation and colour to the girls she marvelled at Ebony's silky hair, but it seemed unfair to say anything when Bridget's was so dry and damaged.

Jenna knew Bridget had little money. She was happy to share.

'I can finish.' Bridget took out a small pouch and applied black eyeliner, black shadow and black lipstick.

With Jenna's parents out for the next few hours the girls were giddy with the freedom of making a noise and doing as they pleased. All three giggled and danced around the room.

Jenna raided her father's garage drinks fridge and brought in a 6-pack of Vodka Cruisers. The girls quickly downed the fruit flavoured drinks, finding a large chunk of bravado, along with a disdain for all rules made by grownups to spoil the fun of kids with responsibilities but no freedom.

'What a waste,' moaned Jenna. 'All this beauty and nowhere to go.'

'The Druid Nails are still playing at *Levi's*. We'd all pass for 18.' Ebony reached into Jenna's wardrobe for a black leather vest.

'Not without ID we wouldn't. Try it on Ebony, go on. Ooh, something red for you Bridget. Here's a mini skirt, it'll look great.'

'Oh thanks.' Bridget grabbed the skirt. 'My brother's friend, Benji, might get us in.'

'All three of us.'

'Won't hurt to try. What have we got to lose?'

Throwing consequences to the wind, along with inevitable parental displeasure, the girls headed to the nightclub. They decided their clothes weren't suitable for bike riding, but found the walk to the nightclub more arduous than they thought. It was also more crowded and more patrolled. Bouncers quickly flicked through ID cards, as well as closely watching incomers.

Bridget had never been near the nightclub and had only met Benji briefly. She knew he haunted the back alleys so she led the girls to a laneway, where a strong smell of beer and urine hung in the air. The girls were not as confident as they'd been on leaving the house, but every time the doors opened and the music pumped out onto the street, their need to be part of the action increased.

Guys came out of the service door, whistled at the girls, gave crude compliments, but didn't offer to let them inside.

'Can you get Benji?' Bridget asked one of the guys. He looked her up and down. Lip curled, he said, 'yeah, you look like his type. He goes for low hanging fruit. I'll see for ya.'

Bridget, having brought her second cruiser with her, took a large gulp and threw the bottle at the bin, missing it.

Benji, annoyed by being interrupted while DJ'ing and servicing his customers with chemical enhancers, was surprised and pleased to see three partly intoxicated teen girls, who looked ready to party. They were his favourite kind of customer. Young, naïve and half drunk. He'd soon fix the rest. He took them inside one by one and told them to keep their distance from each other for a while, so they would avoid detection by the boss (and incidentally make it easier for him to "cut one from the herd"). Benji finished his DJ set and had time to concentrate on his own entertainment.

Jenna and Ebony soon found each other and jived with the crowd.

Bridget stumbled. Benji brought her another drink and put his arm around her, 'just to steady you, my little hottie'.

It wasn't long before Bridget's eyes were smudged, her words slurred and her attempts to find Jenna or Ebony foiled by Benji. Benji's eyes glazed over with lust, this low-hanging fruit was nearly ready. Just one more drink. Something stronger…

But someone else had seen Bridget's state and his intentions were parallel to Benji's, a mountain of a guy. With his height and weight, he was superior to weedy Benji in every way so when "new guy" danced his way over and lifted Bridget onto the dance floor, Benji raised his hands in defeat as the guy placed Bridget's arms around his neck. She held on tight to keep upright. The room was spinning. Her head was pounding. Bile stung the back of her throat.

When the mountain that was holding her upright suggested they go outside for some fresh air, she agreed with a jerking nod.

The guy pushed Bridget up against a wall, gained access to her breasts, gave them bruising kisses and bites, while he attempted to deal with the hidden zip of the borrowed, tight red skirt. Bridget grabbed his hair and yanked his head back, bucked like a mule, kicking him in the groin. She found a broken bottle and held it up to his face as he howled.

'My dad's a cop. You forget, I forget,' she said as he cursed, zipped himself up and walked off, allowing Bridget to slump to the ground where she threw up noisily.

Benji, seeing the sad result, made an anonymous phone call to the police, then took off home. While there, he paced, straining his mental capacity for a way to give himself an alibi, should the police identify him. After an hour of frantic back and forth this possibility seemed so probable that he sincerely regretted phoning the cops, kicked himself for his stupidity and got roaring drunk.

In the police car Bridget realised how much worse the situation could get. Shame increased her silent sobs to cramped regret.

She refused to talk. Her head thundered like a jackhammer. She could think of no one to call to come for her. She struggled to cover her shame, her half-naked spoiled body. The question of next-of-kin brought a harsh cough. Da was in hospital, but that was actually the good news. If only the cops would let her go. But she realised her purse was gone. She didn't even have money for a taxi.

She was given a man's shirt to wear and put in one of the cells, with the door open and an officer seated, writing and keeping watch.

Bridget hugged the shirt around her, lay on the thin mattress, face to the wall and wished to die. She wouldn't have to be around to face this fallout, face the taunts for Shadow Girl. They'd have better words to taunt her with now she'd fallen to this. But not just this, her whole life was one big, messy mistake and there was no way out of it. Everything, from her birth to her current chaos. All bullshit. Nothing. Not even a shadow.

The cops talked of getting a female officer from another station but before they could organise it Bridget told them that her next-of-kin was Leah Bond, a cousin.

Leah dealt with the paperwork quickly, bundled Bridget into her car and took her to the cottage home. Bridget was shaking violently and moaning softly. Leah called a doctor who administered a sedative and left a prescription for the morning-after pill, along with a subtle reminder about the rape clinic and counselling.

In the morning, Leah found a bundle of clothes and a note from Bridget to say that she would return Leah's T-shirt and track pants next time, adding that she didn't need the morning after pill, 'cos nothing like that happened, but thanks a real lot.'

There was a pile of black hair in the bathroom bin. Bridget must have cut her hair, hacked at it by the looks of things.

Leah sighed, but then she realised what a big step it had been for Bridget to reach out to her, even if she hadn't said a word.

The next time Bridget came Leah had prepared sandwiches.

After a plate piled high with sandwiches, Leah brought up the subject of a counsellor.

'But I don't want to go to a shrink. I want to forget, not rehash.' Bridget made her most appealing sad-face.

'You need practice, kid. That's hopeless.' Leah copied Bridget's expression, exaggerating it. 'Anyway, you agreed.'

'I don't remember what I agreed to. I thought it was pizza

on demand.'

'Ha, ha. You know sandwiches is my only kitchen talent.'

'Who could miss that?'

'If you agree to get counselling if I find someone good, I agree that we'll both get tattoos to cover the scars on our wrists.'

'You are so making this all up, Leah.'

'So are you, Bridgeeee. Anyway don't you think tattoos would be good? I hate pain so that's a huge sacrifice for me.'

'What sort of tattoo would we get?'

'You're just changing the subject. I've found a lovely woman who works with the women and girls at the women's shelter.'

Bridget groaned. 'I tell you what, if you cut my hair straight, I'll go. I know you're great with scissors.'

Bridget stood outside the high fence of the women's shelter. This was different. If she'd been taken to a high gloss office she would have been intimidated, but standing there she realized the sacrifice that had been made for the women and children who had temporary residence behind these walls.

She waited. The gate clicked, admitting her to the centre.

Without seeing any of the women residents she was ushered to a cluttered office where an ancient air conditioner coughed.

A woman with a fuller figure introduced herself and offered Bridget a chair. The woman had a swirling skirt and a crimson wrap top. Her hair was held in a bun with a pencil.

Bridget like her instantly.

The woman didn't organise a pad or paperwork. She just listened.

And Bridget, warmed by the less-than-officious surroundings and the woman, talked.

'That night's changed so much. I just mangled my hair. What's with that? My poor hair had nothing to do with it?' Bridget shook her head, wondering why she'd started with something so dumb.

'Women the world over, from the earliest of times have seen their hair as a symbol of their womanhood. It's not an unusual reaction, Bridget.'

'He ... someone, called me "low hanging fruit". As if I was just begging some jerk to do whatever he liked, fuck me, throw me away. Like some drunk slut.'

'I'm not going to ask you to remember and detail what happened that night. That's not how I work and it's not how I believe real healing happens.

'Leah said you'd be different.'

'But there are some other tough questions.' The woman put her elbows on the desk and rested her chin in her hands. 'About your family. There are two things here. Your home life without your mother must be hard and I hope you feel you can talk about that, and the second thing is that it must be hard to forgive your mother.'

Bridget's eyes narrowed. Anger rose, bitter and unexpected. 'What?'

'It's only natural to be angry at feeling abandoned.'

Bridget tensed. 'I'm not angry. I'm not.'

'I'm bringing this up now because there will be things to

face now that your mother has been listed as a missing person and that may affect you. They will question your father, you, your brother. Nothing may come of it—it's been a long time and this has been delayed by your father's claims that she had told him she was leaving.'

The woman paused, waiting for Bridget to catch up.

'You'll have choices, Bridget. If you ever see your mother again you'll have a choice; to reject or accept, forgive or escape. To take the time you have and do something beautiful with it. Build something new out of something old. Don't cry child. Things will get better. It's going to be alright, you'll see.'

Menace

A short, swarthy man in a pin striped suit was seated at a table of the beach outdoor café. Opposite him, sat Brady Harcourt. Brady was enjoying the Sunday beach crowd, waiting for Emma. He couldn't help noticing the bloke. He didn't look like a local or a tourist. Who wore a suit in Noarlunga? On a Sunday?

Brady watched as the stranger in the suit loosened his tie with a wrench and undid a shirt button, then rustled through the local newspaper, not one of the city papers. A bit unusual. The guy took out a pen and busily circled ads in the accommodation section. The suit gave the guy a civilised air, but his demeanour was closed and vigilant. He wouldn't look out of place as a bouncer in a city nightclub, that surly look would work well.

Brady couldn't help wondering what the stranger was doing in Noarlunga. He looked at his watch. Emma would be arriving any minute. She'd gone shopping with Leah Bond, the woman who'd moved into their cul-de-sac.

Shannon Peterson, better known as 'Sharky', didn't like the guy at the table opposite. He seemed to be taking far too much notice of other people, other people in this case being Sharky. Looking down at his suit, he realised he looked pretty stupid. He'd have bought some casual clobber but he hadn't expected to be here long. He'd only brought a backpack and he'd been wearing the suit. He was expected to dress like his boss.

He liked his current lifestyle. Partying with models in Antoine's townhouse, playing bodyguard to beautiful women, and generally lending an air of machismo to Antoine's events by being a burly wingman who deferred to his boss on all occasions. He owed James Antoine. The guy had saved him. Those fraud charges weren't going to go away. Having Antoine step in and pay out his debt had kept his head out of that particular noose. He didn't want to do time again.

Thanks to Leah's sister Stephanie's warning, Antoine had cancelled his Thailand trip, and in less than 24 hours Sharky had slithered his hand into the neighbours' letterbox in Sydney and found mysterious mail with two addresses, the neighbours' and c/- Noarlunga Post Office. In one of the envelopes was a Qantas cheque refunding her flight to Perth due to an unplanned detour relating to stormy weather, noting her change of mind option to travel to Adelaide. The letter was in the name of the neighbour but it was clearly Leah's mail. Gotcha! Sharky and Antoine had flown to Adelaide and interrogated everyone getting off the plane, including Adam Price, whose height and demeanour had Antoine yanking at his sweaty collar. His patience strained, Antoine sent Sharky to Noarlunga while he flew back to Sydney.

Leah Antoine had vanished into thin air, and he, Sharky

Peterson, had to find her and get her back.

Why was Antoine so fixated on this bird? Maybe the broad was Antoine's meal ticket. Now that, he could understand. He'd have no qualms about roughing her up in that case. That wouldn't bother him. Women needed to be reminded who was in charge every now and then anyway.

Ah, if this was about money it would explain his last phone call to Antoine. He'd been instructed to leave his fancy hotel and find a cheap motel. It would also explain why Antoine sent Sharky instead of the expensive Private Investigator he'd hired. Sharky was already on the payroll. A twinge of resentment kicked in. He'd better be well rewarded for this caper.

He usually liked his job, but he was tired and irritable and this place was getting to him. The locals were a tight bunch and even though he'd been here for weeks he hadn't turned up anything. This blending in and making polite conversation with country hicks wasn't his style. It was one thing to accompany Antoine on his rock star lifestyle, but it was altogether another thing having to cross the country to check out some lead on his boss's ex.

Hang on, there was a blonde woman crossing the road, short spiky hair. He became instantly alert. The blonde was wearing sunglasses. She was coming closer. He didn't take his eyes off her. There was a brunette with her, but he kept his eyes on the blonde. The blonde came closer. His heart raced. The thrill of the hunt kicked in; near but so far. He pulled his hat down over his eyes, glad of the dark glasses.

Sharky was sure it was Leah. She was approaching the man

at the nearby table. He'd soon get a good look at her. If only she'd take those huge sunglasses off. She must have read his mind because that's just what she did as she beamed at the man. It wasn't Leah, but the woman was a dead ringer for her. Cursing under his breath he stood up. Damn, he'd been so sure. Maybe he was too desperate.

He picked up the newspaper ready to move away when he noticed the brunette. She was standing stock-still in shock, staring straight at him. He narrowed his eyes. Why was she reacting like that? Then it hit him like a soccer punch in the solar plexus. The brunette was Leah Antoine. Different hair and clothes, but the same full lips and huge eyes.

The blonde turned to Leah, registered Leah's fear and slowly turned to look at Sharky. He saw a protective, fierce look in the blonde woman's eyes. She took a step towards him.

Leah took a step back. The man at the table was now watching like a hawk. The raw fear in Leah's eyes had given her away; Sharky would never have noticed her apart from her reaction. Never recognised her.

Now the man stood, and as he walked towards Sharky, the blonde took out her mobile and held it up. Crap, she was videoing him. His elation at finding Leah evaporated. He was supposed to track her down and approach her discreetly with no-one around. He should have stayed seated. He'd blown his cover, and his one chance. This was going all wrong. Antoine would be furious.

Sharky Peterson bolted across the road, climbed into his sleek black hire car and spun off.

Leah trembled violently.

'Leah, are you alright. Who was that? James?' asked Emma.

'No, his bodyguard, his henchman. Sent to sort me out. Oh God, that means James knows where I am.' Then Leah ran wildly across the road towards Bren and John's.

'What was all that about?' asked Brady. 'Did you know that guy?'

'No, but Leah certainly did,' said Emma. She sighed, then realising that it was time to let Brady in on the story, continued, 'she escaped a brutal marriage. She's been hiding out here.'

'Oh my God, the poor thing! No wonder she has a hunted look. She has just moved. What timing! She won't feel safe now.'

'No, she won't. Brady, you're not angry that I didn't tell you?'

'Of course not. You had to protect her identity. What will happen? Bloody dangerous looking guy. We should have phoned the police.'

'She didn't give us a chance. She'll go to Bren's, maybe Bren can talk some sense into her. Get her to contact the police. She couldn't be in better hands. She hasn't wanted to take any action, but I don't think she has much choice now. At least I have photos. They might help.'

'Do you want to go to her? I'll understand. Honestly.'

'I will later. I'll wait for her to phone.' Emma sat down and looked out to sea, clearly shaken.

'Are you okay, Emma?'

'I'll be fine, thanks Brady. You looked like you were ready to shirtfront him.'

'I will forever regret that I didn't do just that.'

It's time

'Oh, Bren, I don't know what to do ... I hate coming to you but ...' Leah shook violently as Bren ushered her inside.

'You were so right to come, honey,' said Bren, 'We feel like family.'

'But you have enough without my ... fiasco ...'

'You are not a fiasco, you are a very dear friend. Oh sweetie, here...' Bren embraced a trembling Leah.

John stood silently in the kitchen doorway.

'Get us a pot of tea, will you darling?' said Bren.

'No worries,' said John, padding barefoot into the kitchen. He expertly flipped the kettle on and began to set out the tea service tray, filling the jug with sugar and setting the cups along the bench. Bren hid her surprise. It had been a long time since John had taken over the tea rituals. She was even more stunned when he sat down at the table. 'Who is this guy threatening you?' he asked, looking directly at Leah.

Bren leaned back in the dining room chair as she watched

John unravel the layers of Leah's disastrous day with calm deliberation. It was man's business now. This was the old John.

Leah spoke clearly, laying out the facts. The only sign of her agitation was the constant twisting of her hands.

'I hope you're prepared to do something, Leah. I have had you pegged as made of sterner stuff and I'm sure you realise what has to be done.' John's voice was steely.

'Well, I ... I'm not sure what to do ... I ... phoned the police once, and it made things worse.'

'Well, it is a police matter. Stalking, threats and assault.'

'But Sharky didn't say anything ...'

'You think that man was here for a spot of sight-seeing? Really, Leah.' John stood with hands on hips.

Bren blanched at John's tough approach, but kept her peace.

'But what can the police do? It's ...'

'Well, you'll never know until you go to them and tell the whole story. It's different this time. Emma took photos, you say? She'll stand by you and so will we. Bren will lend you a coat. It's getting chilly.'

Bren and Leah were stunned, but John was on his feet.

The new head police officer, Sergeant Peter Benson, showed none of the agitation Leah was experiencing. He acted as if he was taking a dinner order, so calm was his manner. It was immensely reassuring. As soon as he heard the tale of Antoine's henchman he brought the three of them through into an interview room. His questions became sharper. What was Sharky's real name? His address? His history? What role did he play for James Antoine?

Emma arrived and was ushered into the room. 'I videoed the whole thing, well, most of it. I caught the part where he approached Leah. I'm Emma Harcourt.'

'I'll need a statement from you too. And we'll take a copy of that video—most helpful.'

'Hey Clamont,' he called out. A young officer entered. 'Everything settled from that accident? Run this name for me. I think this guy's got form and he might still be in town, or nearby. Hotels, motels…'

'No worries Serg, I'll get right on it. Irish is on the accident.'

'Right then, would you people like to take a seat while I get some paperwork sorted. I'll give you an event number for today, m'dear. Don't lose it. But you need to apply for Apprehended Violence Orders against both men pronto, the husband and the sidekick.'

'Don't I need a solicitor?' asked Leah.

'Not for an AVO in this case, we can do interim orders, then pass it on to the magistrate as a matter of urgency. Make an appointment first thing Monday morning with the Chamber Magistrate at the local court. He'll take down all the details and set things in motion. You need to do this. A duty solicitor will assist you on the day. Of course if you have your own solicitor, that's okay, you'll need one sooner rather than later. You need to untangle yourself from this man in every possible way as soon as possible. Do you understand?'

'Yes,' said Leah.

'I hope you mean that, m'dear, because we cops get sick of women who protect the men who harm them and end up being the ones to break the AVOs. Don't worry about your husband. The court will grant an AVO ex-parte, that means he won't have to attend. You'll be safe. You are safe now. How long have you been away from him?'

'I've been here five months, but we lived apart for months before.'

'And he still didn't leave you alone then, did he? That's why you went into hiding. You're going to have to face this guy down. Men who hit women are cowards and until you show your husband he has no power he'll keep coming, and coming. An AVO is your first step.'

'I've always worried an AVO would make things worse ... you see the news ... and ...'

'The news only reports the failed cases, which are rare. Trust me. I'm here to tell you that an AVO works more than 90% of the time, and even then breaches are usually begging and apologetic advances, flowers and the like. The media doesn't show the whole picture. Most men are terrified of their image, their career. Like I said, cowards. I've personally wasted too much time trying to talk angry idiots down to the pavement, when I should've been taking them straight into custody. If they break the AVO, they break the law. Simple as that.'

Leah grew pale. 'I didn't know that. I won't be one of the ones who back down,' she said with new conviction.

'Good girl.' The sergeant smiled, then walked away to confer with the other officer. In only minutes the paperwork had been attended and a card with the officer's name pressed into Leah's hand. 'Please, do not hesitate to phone us at any time if you see either of these men, or are contacted by them in any manner.'

'I will,' said Leah.

'I think it would be wise for you to stay with your friends, just for tonight.'

'She'll be fine with us,' said John.

Bren touched Leah's shoulder. 'That's a good idea, Leah.'

Leah turned to the officers. 'Will ... will you be able to tell me what happens with Sharky? Is that ... Just so I know if I'm safe ... um ...'

'We'll phone when we know something, but he has probably high-tailed it to the airport. He may have had a hire car. He has a warrant out. We're looking forward to making the acquaintance of Mr. Shannon Peterson in the very near future and organising new accommodation for him. And as for you, m'dear, good luck.'

Once outside the police station in the cool evening air, Bren threw her coat over Leah's shoulders.

John continued to take the lead, ushering the women to the car with manly concern that brought tears to Bren's eyes. Was John finally emerging from the shadow of depression?

'You're staying with us Leah, okay,' John said, opening the car door. When they arrived home he took their order for a pizza delivery, ignoring the protests of the women. They sat at the dining table with a new pot of tea. John had vetoed coffee, amusing Leah.

'I do love a masterful man,' said Bren, winking at him.

John smiled.

Leah's face had lost its lined and taut look. 'I'd never have believed a visit to the police station could make me calm. I've feared involving them for years. I can't thank you enough. I really want to act now. I feel strangely empowered. I'll look for a solicitor straight away.'

'Do you still have the business card? For that lovely Adam Price?' asked Bren.

Leah smiled. 'Dr Seuss? Oh, I couldn't...'

Bren raised an eyebrow. 'Dr Seuss, hey? Nicknames already.'

'I have it.' Leah fumbled through her purse and found the card.

'Yes, you're right.' Leah's eyes filled with tears. John already had the phone outstretched to give her. 'But it's the weekend...'

'Listen, honey,' said John, 'if a man gives you his mobile number, he means you to use it.'

Bren laughed. 'Who knew you were the expert, John?'

'I've been around.'

'That's a *very* impertinent grin, John Burnside. I shall have to interrogate you further.' Bren didn't noticed Leah leave the room with the phone.

'Let her be, Bren. She's going to be okay now.'

'And how do you know that, Mr Expert?'

'She's finally facing the past.'

Bren's eyes were full of hope as she held John's direct gaze.

'Yes, Bren. It's a lesson to me too. It won't be easy; or quick, but it's time I came home.'

Bren threw herself into his embrace.

Leah padded silently into the other room and dialled the number on the card.

Reaching

'Adam Price speaking.'

Adam put his bacon and cheese bagel back on the paper bag carefully. It wouldn't do to have his secretary, Delia, know about his weekends at the office, although he swore the woman was psychic.

'Leah, Leah Bond, how marvellous ... No ... no bother, don't mention it ... Oh dear ... start at the beginning ... I knew there was something, but I never imagined; poor love ... No, I will *not* recommend a local man ... I'll be there ... Stop thanking me. Of course, you'll need an appointment in my office, here in Glenelg, Send me what you have, details, dates etc., ... I'm glad John and Bren are there for you ... I've been meaning to call in on them, and ... - well, it's lovely to hear your voice, Leah ... No, truly, it's not that much ... Wow, you are ready to go ... Let me do it all for you, please ... Get some rest ... Bye to you too.'

The lethargy that had dogged Adam for the past months vanished as he flipped through files and hastily wrote instructions for Delia.

He couldn't explain, even to himself, why he felt such urgency to reach Leah's side. He knew it was more than a masculine urge to protect, but he didn't want to analyse it, there was too much to do. Anyway, answers would come when he saw Leah again. He would either lay to rest his fascination for her, or ... who knew?

He slammed the office door a little more emphatically than he intended. The lift took forever, so he bounded down the fire stairs.

Court, AVOs, henchmen with warrants, solicitors. And now a shrink, some Dr Kent. As Leah lay in Bren and John's guest room she wondered how her life had come to this. Even more astonishing was the fact that she felt more at peace than she had for a long time. For the first time, she had not only the law on her side, but people, good people.

A memory of Adam Price flickered through her mind. A bubble had burst inside her, and it whispered of things to come. Fear had been her enemy for so long she hadn't allowed for the possibility that fear was a greater foe than James.

But it wasn't James that filled her thoughts later.

Watching the mirrored glow of the low lamplight in the window, Leah replayed every word of her conversations with Adam Price. With forgotten yearning she clung to the cadences in his voice. The care. There had been a spark between them in Melbourne, but she had pushed it aside, denied it.

She was no longer able to ignore it, so she indulged the wonder of that indefinable tug between a man and a woman.

Willow

Willow sat with her legs curled under her in the red chesterfield settee in the manner of a dancer with the ability to curve comfortably anywhere at all.

She finally had her mother to herself after the chaotic manner in which they had met, a woman known locally as the town gossip.

Willow felt bad about that day. She'd rehearsed her role as a shockingly bogan woman, in order to test her mother. A mother she'd thought about for 28 years. Before they met, Willow had done her homework on her mother, chatting quietly with unsuspecting town people.

In spite of Mrs Wainwright's public life she was described as "not what you'd call a people person". Her considerable energy had been aimed at enhancing her husband, Earl's career. She'd taken over the running of their dry-cleaning business to allow him to scale the ladder of success.

Willow had expected her mother to send her packing,

reinforcing her perception that her mother hadn't wanted her and was a stuck up cow, one of the coarser comments made by "the public". But Prudence had welcomed her daughter and told her to call her mother, or Prudence, whatever Willow was comfortable with.

This attitude, and the warmth in the home, had given Willow feelings of guilt for her earlier behaviour as she desperately attempted to connect to her mother.

However, Prudence seemed unable to follow the simplest of conversations. She hadn't been herself since the heart attack, a common enough phenomena for those who have come face to face with the grim reaper.

Sitting with her only child in the soft glow of the afternoon sun, Prudence became nostalgic. However, not for the child perched on the settee near her, but a thousand other things that made no sense, not even to her long-suffering husband Earl.

Earl Wainwright watched as Willow tried to connect with her biological mother, seeking answers for those important questions that arise with a child adopted out. Willow knew that Prudence hadn't been a teenage mother, she'd been 28, the age Willow was now. Certainly an age where considerations for giving up a child would be somewhat different to the decisions made by a frantic teenager.

Prudence was currently rambling on about the dry-cleaning business. A business they had sold several years ago because it had all been too much, according to Prudence. Earl didn't mind one way or the other. She'd been an astute, well-respected businesswoman. She was currently obsessed with past employees, in particular a woman named Jean with whom she'd developed a close friendship.

Apparently Prudence had some task to do for Jean, whoever Jean was. It was a task that she'd forgotten, but was now obsessed about.

Willow gave up trying to steer Prudence to the subject of her past, and the baby she relinquished to a "fine young couple from Sydney's northern suburbs". This was the only piece of information she'd shared so far. And, so like the woman herself, it was an attempt to direct the listener to her benevolent nature. One that perhaps existed only in her imagination.

Earl, wishing he had the facts to give Willow, brought his chair closer and asked her to tell him about her life, her adoptive parents, had she been happy? This was the one question Willow had dreamed and hoped for, and having it spoken out loud had the effect of bringing salty tears to her eyes.

When Willow had been handed to the desperate pair who couldn't have children of her own, she had been a beautiful babe with pale skin and just a fluffy hint of hair. No one would have suspected that her parentage included an African AmEarlan man.

This was a fact considered unnecessary by Prudence who had favoured the idea of a private adoption for the purpose of being able to keep the background and reasons for the adoption to a minimum. No lengthy forms or paperwork. Just a birth certificate with father unknown and the incredible gift of a child, without the dreadful waiting periods experienced by other parents desperate to adopt.

The couple were elated, they had their own secrets. They were deemed too old to adopt and were thrilled to bypass the red tape and endless questions. Like many older parents their experience of raising children was sparse indeed and a lively child had tested their patience. Things deteriorated when the child's skin darkened to a degree that was impossible to pass off as tanned, and her hair grew into a tangled, red afro. There were no mixed race children at their local playgroup, and this child with dusty brown skin and a fizz of red hair became an embarrassment. At the age of three, Willow entered the foster system where she felt more out of place than ever.

Naturally, Willow had always felt she was not good enough—the first reaction of children the world over. What was wrong with me?

Willow had expected her biological mother to reinforce this notion and in that expectation Willow was not entirely disappointed, but what she hadn't been prepared for was the warmth and joy she found in Earl Wainwright. A response so open and spontaneous it surprised Willow more than anything else ever had. It wasn't as if she would be considered a boon to his life, public or otherwise. It was as pure and simple as love should be.

As Willow shared her story of being different, feeling inferior, Earl blew his nose, wiped his eyes and shook his head.

'I don't know how anyone, anyone at all could treat a beautiful gift that way. If only we'd, we'd known sooner. That must have been awful. But here you are now...' Earl leaned hopefully towards Willow. 'It is my absolute delight to call you daughter.'

Willow spoke about how her university years had changed her perspective. She hadn't been different there, hadn't been scorned or rejected. Everyone was different and all the flavours were celebrated. She'd excelled at her studies and become an occupational therapist who loved her work.

'Your father? Have you wanted to find him? I'm sorry I can't help with that. She told me nothing.'

'I don't know. I guess I'd like to know who he was.'

Prudence nodded here and there, gave a distracted 'hmm', an 'aha', then surprised the other two by sitting forward wide-eyed.

'Earl, it was the day I brought home that horrible big black car, you know, the one you hated.' Prue narrowed her eyes and held Earl's gaze. 'That was the day.'

'I see,' said Earl, seeing nothing. 'That black car.'

'I made a promise that day, Earl.'

'To take the car back. I remember, Prue.'

'No! no! Not that. She, she… oh darn… why can't I remember.' Prudence slumped in the chair. 'She was waiting for a taxi, but it passed her by. I told our driver to go back, but he, he… that man, blast!'

'Rest Prue, you're tired. Do you want to go to bed?'

'Not yet. I enjoy listening to the two of you.'

Earl bent and kissed her.

'I was never good enough for you, Earl.'

'Don't be silly my love. You made me what I am.'

'Tosh,' said Prudence, 'how you do go on.' She looked at

Willow, reached out a trembling arm.

Willow kissed her hand, tears welling.

'I gave you a beautiful daughter though, didn't I Earl.'

'You did indeed, Prue, you did indeed.'

Prudence's eyes tried to focus, then fluttered. Soft snoring followed.

Willow and Earl decided that it was time for snacks.

'I make excellent pancakes,' said Earl.

'Does that classify as a snack, Earl?'

'Tonight it does.'

As the two of them debated over batter consistency and what type of flour was best, where was the maple syrup, no, not lemon—an hour had passed.

And Prudence Anne Wainwright had taken her last breath in the recliner chair that matched the red chesterfield settee. She'd always thought she would take the secret of her daughter to her grave, but it was another secret entirely that went there with her. One she had been trying to remember and fulfil.

Funereal weather

Most of the town had been sleeping in their beds when Prudence Wainwright died. Every death has a different response. Popular people are mourned deeply, celebrities are mourned as if they were known friends. People who are often described as "larger than life" leave a shock in their passing. If it could happen to them...

No one could imagine the town without Prudence Wainwright and the turnout at her funeral and wake was remarked on by all.

Brady and Emma Harcourt sat in their kitchen while the three girls binged on Netflix and chocolate covered pretzels. It was the longest Bridget had stayed at their place. It had occurred to Emma that Mrs Wainwright might need a live-in companion and that Bridget might fit the bill. After all, Willow had moved in with her toddler and might also be grateful for someone around the house.

All that changed with the morning news.

Instead, along with the rest of the town, Emma wrote condolence cards to Earl, Willow & family.

Willow, who'd never felt a part of any family, didn't know what to do, or where to start. She'd managed her mother's hospitalization but that had involved very little. Was she expected to host a wake? Just what would be expected of her?

Earl made it very clear that he wanted her to stay in the granny flat downstairs. It was her home. The problem of a wake was taken care of by the Pearl Ladies Inc. a charity group where Prudence had been a member. The Pearl Ladies held events to raise funds for various local associations and were more than happy to put on a high tea.

While Willow wondered what a high tea was, Earl made the decision that there would only be a graveside service with the wake held at the community hall. Being a Person of Public Importance, as Prudence often called him, didn't mean he wanted a public occasion for the funeral of his wife of thirty plus years.

The sky opened on the day of the funeral, bucketing down with a ferocity seldom seen for that time of year and place. It denied Prudence Wainwright her last chance for public admiration. Mourners ran for shelter. Many were caught out. Only a few had brought umbrellas. This rare event made for a short service indeed. The rain stayed for a week.

The dense, dark clouds that accompanied the downpour seemed to permeate every room of the Wainwright house. Willow retreated, hollow eyed and silent.

'Willow. We must talk.' Earl sat at the dining table.

Willow, expecting to be cast adrift yet again, sat at the farthest end of the table and crossed her arms.

'You've been so silent, so distant. Is everything alright. I know it's been a shock, sweetie, but...'

'It's my fault. If I hadn't come. If I hadn't tricked her with my bogan, hippy nonsense. If I'd just...'

'Don't, please, Willow. It's just not true.'

'I didn't even really connect with her. I sent her into shock. A shock that killed her.'

'You mustn't think that. It isn't true. Come sit here.' Earl patted the table opposite him, brought out a plastic ice cream container.

'This box has Prudence's mediations.' Earl placed one Webster pack then two, then three on the table.

'Gosh,' said Willow. 'There are so many pills left. Aren't they, shouldn't they be empty?'

'I didn't notice. But for a long time Prue hadn't been taking her medications, her heart pill.' He pointed at a small blue pill, 'her blood pressure tablet. I should have been paying attention. If I had...'

'Oh, Mr Wainwright, you mustn't think that.'

Earl leant back and folded his arms, and smiled.

'Oh, I see what you're doing.' Willow's lips twitched.

'And the nurses in Intensive Care told me that Prue was muttering about some woman, this Jean she keeps talking about, kept talking about. So nobody knows. What I want you to remember, my new daughter, are the last words Prue said, do you remember?'

'The last... um.'

'I will tell you. "I gave you a beautiful daughter, didn't I Earl." Those were her last words. To you and to me. So can we please go on as we intended. As father and grandfather, daughter and grandson.'

Clearing the house was far more daunting for Earl than clearing the air with Willow.

He left the master bedroom and slept in a guest room, putting off the day he'd have to sort through his wife's possessions. When he did decide it was time, it was such a stop-start venture that he thought he'd never be able to properly face it.

He'd only managed to tackle one drawer of his wife's dressing table. He found slips of paper with names and numbers, dates and times all through her top drawer where makeup had spilled, leaving puffs of powder, tissues with pink stains and bottles of perfume without lids.

There was nothing about any Jean.

Finding a box, he placed all the papers into it, then threw the rest out, rightly guessing that he had thrown out cosmetics worth a king's ransom.

The photographs of the funeral arrived, there were business papers to see to, and joint bank accounts to deal with, along with funeral expenses.

He went back to work two weeks later.

Willow gained a part time job at the hospital, and life took on a new rhythm.

Glenelg

Leah's appointment with Adam Price came around sooner than she'd thought. She'd given him the details he'd need to represent her. She had dates and times but didn't have her marriage certificate, something she'd discussed with Adam in their frequent, long phone calls.

Adam hadn't pressed her to take action on the divorce, but was pleased she had AVOs against James and Sharky.

Delia, Adam's receptionist had made the appointment with Leah only a few days after her conversation with Adam. The woman introduced herself and chatted to Leah as if she knew her. Had Adam talked about her? The possibility gave a frisson of delight. Delia said Adam was attending a conference at the Stamford at Brighton and Leah could see him afterwards.

Bridget had slept over the night before and Leah decided a day out would be a treat for the shy girl, give her something else to think about, somewhere else to be.

At first Bridget had hesitated.

'I only want to help, Bridget.'

'You?'

'Of course me! I'm your cousin aren't I?' Leah smiled.

'Ha ha. Cousin. I can't believe the cops fell for that.' Bridget wiped a sleeve across her eyes. Bridget's eyes met Leah's. 'Your guy ... ah, man ... won't mind.'

'His name is Adam. He's not precisely mine.'

'Well, if the hours you spend on the phone mean anything, he's more than a friend and I don't want to get in the way, he probably doesn't need a hot mess like me hanging around.'

'If he could handle my past, trust me, he can handle anything.'

Leah was rewarded with a wan smile.

They caught the 8:47 am train. They planned to journey together and part on arrival.

Remembering her student days in Sydney, Leah was strangely elated about the journey. She'd loved train travel then and the trip from Melbourne with Bren and John had reignited that joy.

As for Bridget she was fascinated with every new vista.

The train driver had been a narrator in a past life; his mellow accent and cheery announcements added a whimsical touch. He announced the location and rules for the 'quiet carriages'.

Bridget explained what a quiet carriage was. Leah was amazed; what a wonderful idea! They made their way to the quiet carriage. Leah was glad they'd no longer have to sit opposite young parents with a cute wriggling bub. The vision of the trio had renewed an ache in her own heart.

While Bridget read a book with a baseball hat down over her face, Leah sat with a slim older woman whose Asian heritage had given her 'that kind of beauty'. The woman and her husband were happily retired. She spoke of the freedom of having the children leave home, the freedom of new life and interests.

Leah was warmed by another kind of freedom, the freedom of conversing with a stranger, where the marvellous ability to connect had replaced her former instincts to hide. Her life was taking a new open direction. A memory twinkled. Adam Price had been the first to walk through that door.

When Bridget and Leah exited at Marion Station. Leah headed for the library where she'd be free to email and catch up with her fashion business.

Bridget hesitated at the exit. She had travelled by train before but it had been on school excursions so the destination and the activities had been regulated. For a few blinding seconds she was tempted to get straight back on the train. Then she shook herself and headed out of the station.

The park in front of her was beautiful, even with the sharp angles of the city and its glass buildings. She took a few photos, not caring if she looked like a tourist. There was so many images that would inspire her art later. It was time to move beyond cemetery views and scrubland. She had her school final artwork piece to complete, and there was a scholarship.

No one other than Leah knew where she was and that gave

her a new feeling of safety. So this day, she would be observer.

She arrived at the first set of lights where there were two classes of people anxious to cross the street—those who took green walking signs seriously and those who didn't. The first group were fooled into starting onto the street every time one of the 'I don't care for green lights' people crossed. One girl had several false starts, but obediently returned to the curb when she realised that the person loping across the road was a lawless individual.

There were shops with pristine windows and glossy beige porcelain mannequins posed precisely, while wearing the latest Chanel creations. One boutique beauty salon offered 'clip-on eyelashes', which seemed as sensible as using 3 inch building nails as heels on shoes. Another clinic offered facial rejuvenation which would have been a lot more convincing if the model was older than 20. There were men in slick suits with perfect haircuts and ties that would never have dared to slip sideways. They were oblivious to the world and possessed an amazing talent to manoeuvre through the crowded streets while totally engrossed in their mobile devices.

Bridget entered the Mockingbird Café that Leah had heard was divine. A young waitress arrived with pad open and pen at the ready.

'I'll have a hot chocolate,' said Bridget, shrugging at the ordinariness of her request.

'What kind of chocolate?' asked the young brunette. 'The house special?

'Ah yes?' said Bridget.

It was liquid velvet.

She ordered a light lunch and a Portuguese tart, then lost herself in the book-lined walls.

She had the choice of waiting for Leah at the Stamford or catching the train. Massaging her aching feet she decided on the Stamford. Opulence had a new face there. Bridget was dazzled. Designer clothes walked by—a purple jacket with fastidious overstitching, shiny yellow patent leather heels a mile high. Necklace beads, black and shiny, as large as conch shells adorned an orange coat. Black stockings were de rigeur. Everywhere there was magnificence.

The black and white tiled floor shone like diamonds. Acres of pristine glass welcomed light and shielded from noise. There was a narrow, embarrassed line of worn floorboards, hoping to be unnoticed. Men with briefcases on wheels glided confidently, with sleek slashes of steel-grey hair, nonchalant charm and brief, breezy conversation.

Attentive service personnel blended with discreet security. Men sat on large latte-coloured ottomans absorbed with technology. Perfectly coiffed women brunched; chatting cheerfully, licking delicate fingers for the last taste of exotic treats while they sipped tea in elegant cups. Footsteps echoed quietly on parquet floors. Soft down lights glowed. A stylish rug ran the length of the foyer.

In the centre of the foyer was a sumptuous arrangement of silk flowers, glass vases under a modern circular chandelier. Bridget was amused when gleaming chrome luggage trolleys passed with only a handbag on board.

Revived by an extremely expensive cup of tea, Bridget decided to catch the train home. It was several hours before

Leah would be free.

Using the last of her money for a taxi, Bridget arrived at Leah's cottage, found the hidden key left for her, and let herself in.

Images of vibrant colours, oblique angles and cityscape architecture flitted through her mind, and a myriad of faces had captured her mind and ignited a passion.

She spent the next few hours frenetically sketching until hunger overcame her and she made a cheese sandwich with thick tasty cheese and fresh crusty bread, butter instead of oily cheap margarine.

Heaven. How would she ever repay Leah for this home, this safe place, this haven? Wishing she could stay, Bridget left her artwork on the table and walked back to the place she called home. Home that was a prison with a deranged warden.

We meet again

At the Stamford, Leah entered the foyer. She glanced at her watch. She had half an hour before meeting Adam.

Everything glittered and shone. Leah was no stranger to opulence, but she'd rarely stopped to take it in. She walked upstairs on lush burgundy carpet and was directed to a lift. The conference room appeared deserted. Slipping off her coat, she wandered straight into the arms of Adam Price.

Adam swallowed hard. Nothing could have prepared him for the vision in his arms. Setting himself up with a perfect vantage point to see her arrive had done no good, no good at all. She had slipped out onto the one area he himself found serene, the outdoor garden. Entranced by the garden she hadn't seen him either, which was why she was now locked in the arms he'd automatically put out to steady her. She looked so different from the woman on the plane. Until he looked into her eyes. Warm honey flowed through him.

'Hello, Suess,' she said, still standing in his embrace.

'Hello, yourself,' he said, holding her gaze.

'Your secretary is wonderful, Adam. Is she your mother?'

'Oh dear, what did she say?'

'Ah, where do I start? Let's put it this way, she gave me full disclosure.'

'I'll dock her pay.'

'I'm kidding, she didn't say much ...'

'You know Leah Bond—if I didn't know any better I'd say you were teasing me.'

'It's been so long I don't know myself ... but if I was ...'

'...if you were?' Adam stepped slowly back, taking Leah with him. She matched him step for step until they reached the cool shelter of a stucco wall.

His breath quickening, he caressed the tendrils of her hair and was rewarded with a contented sigh. Taking his time, he massaged her neck with slow, gentle fingers. His eyes were alert to her mood. He didn't want to rush things. He'd had no intention of making any moves on her; his reaction to her had taken him by surprise.

He realised all those long conversations to her had been slowly awakening something lost, something both sensual and sacred. Too sacred for hasty fumbling or hurried passion. With the current trauma in her life, he owed her respect, time. He couldn't escape the connecting of their souls as they had laid bare their secrets and pains. The very circumstances that brought them together had also ensured that there would be no pretence between them, no barriers, but he wanted this to last.

He could wait. Lifting her chin he slowed the seduction of

his fingers and brought his lips to touch hers. It was lighter than a feather and something within soared when she leant forward after he'd ended the brief kiss. 'I can't be your solicitor,' he said, cupping her face, fearing her reaction.

'I know,' she said, 'I came here to sack you.'

He laughed. 'Oh, great, and I thought you trusted me.'

'I do.'

'Say that again.'

'I do.'

'Again.'

'Adam, really! What on earth ...?'

'You might need to practice that, Leah. Never know when you might need those words.'

'Adam?' Wha ...'

'I'm falling in love with you, Leah Bond/Antoine, and I don't intend to unfall.'

She giggled. 'Unfall? That's not a word Dr Seuss.'

''Tis now.' He kissed her again.

When Leah had regained her ragged breathing, she touched his face. 'I don't want to unfall either.'

Two huge windowed-walls allowed brilliant morning light into the hotel room. With a silk sheet wrapped carelessly around her, Leah bit into a croissant with delight. 'This is heaven.' She licked her lips.

'Why thank you,' said Adam, throwing a robe over broad shoulders and sitting beside her.

Leah gave him a gentle shove.

He lay splayed on the bed and pulled her down to him.

'I meant the croissant, Dr Seuss. Who knew chocolate was an ideal breakfast food.'

'I thought you had lived the high life and experienced all of this many times, Ms Not Yourself.'

'I guess that's the impression, but it wasn't like that. I didn't even see that much of James. He was constantly off to Thailand to his businesses. His business partner was our marriage celebrant for our beach wedding.'

'Ah. The inevitable intrudes.' Adam was suddenly serious. 'This is not going to be easy to hear, Leah.'

Leah put down the croissant. Her heart thundered. Could there truly be more bad news?

'James has fled to Thailand. He was implicated in Sharky's criminal activities and had a few of his own.'

'Well, that's not a surprise is it?'

'No, but this will be. Your marriage to James was a sham, actually more a scam. It was fake. It wasn't legal. It was part of an elaborate con for your money. The woman celebrant was part of that.'

'But there were people there, and, oh my God. They could have been anyone. There were none of my friends, only Stephanie, who was very much taken with James. And there were flowers and, oh my God. He gave me an ultimatum. Here and now, or never.'

'You were only eighteen and without parents. You were an easy...'

'...target. Of course I was. Stupid, stupid. What a fool?'

Adam wrapped his arms around her as she sobbed.

'Was anything real?' Leah held her hands over her face.

'Anything at all?'

Adam watched her silently, feeling her pain at being so used by a man she had loved and trusted.

'This seems worse,' she said, 'I don't know why. What can I trust?'

'I advise that you take your time, take all this in. And it would probably be a good idea to have the point of view that anything James could have told you, is most likely a lie.'

Leah stood and walked to the window. As beautiful as the night had been and the scene before her, she felt numb. And the only person she wanted, needed was her sister, Stephanie.

She must have whispered Stephanie's name because Adam, beautiful Adam, handed her the phone.

Unable to speak to Stephanie, Leah left a message with her phone number and address. Hiding was no longer necessary. But how would Stephanie react?

Turning to Adam she asked, 'so that's the end of court?'

'For you, we hope, but you might be called as a witness for James or Sharky. James might be extradited, depending on whether his crimes were committed in Australia.'

Leah slumped back on the bed. Would this nightmare never end?

Believed

Stephanie slid effortlessly out of the taxi, clutching her Gucci handbag. A sharp city suit made her stand out from the beachside crowd, but Stephanie Bond had never cared one whit what anyone thought. Refusing to step aside for the bikini clad skaters and the tanned laughing boys in board shorts, she lowered her designer sunglasses a fraction to look around.

So this is where her younger sister had chosen to hide out. At least it wasn't a dusty outback town or a tiny country village with a one bowser petrol station, rangy dogs, dry dusty roads and brown grass. She didn't know what she'd been expecting, but it wasn't this.

Stephanie paused. A warm, sultry breeze carried salt air, and the crashing of the surf caught her attention. The taxi had dropped her near the bus station. The beach was only a hundred metres away. Looking across to the other side of the road Stephanie saw the street café where Leah might share many meals with her new friends, in her new life. She crossed the quiet street, only stopping briefly on the traffic island before taking a seat in the outdoor area of the Blue Reef Café. After ordering a skim latte, she settled back and took in the whole panorama. It was amazing. No wonder Leah had chosen this place.

In the early days, before Liandra's confession Stephanie couldn't comprehend how Leah was able to turn her back on her life as a darling of the fashion industry, the world at her feet. Stephanie knew Leah felt guilty that her sudden disappearance had left her sister with the fallout just days before the Summer Collection Fashion Show.

'Why, Leah? I don't understand ...' said Stephanie.

'Please, Stephanie. I don't have time. I have to go *now*. Can't you just accept that? Just look after the books like you always have. I'll be in touch ... My assistant Jill will oversee models & outfits at the Fashion Show. All I want you to do is attend in my place and declare the event open. Just. Don't. Tell. James.'

To Stephanie the message seemed garbled. 'Surely you could have stayed for the show. What are a few days in the scheme of things? Where is all this coming from? You and James are the perfect couple with the perfect life, what do you expect me to say to people? This is irresponsible, it's not like you. What am I supposed to say to James? 'Hey, I'm in charge of everything now. He'll love that!' Stephanie said.

Leah had wept like a child. 'James will not attend and will no longer be involved ...'

This blunt statement only added to Stephanie's confusion. 'You're a coward, Leah.'

Those words haunted Stephanie as she sat on the bench. Would Leah want to see her? Would she pack up and run again? She wouldn't blame Leah if she never trusted her again.

Setting things right had taken longer than Stephanie thought. Not only had James been manhandling the models, he'd been 'creatively' making claims on the finances. Stephanie had quietly ousted James completely.

Stephanie felt shame wash over her. Her last conversation with Leah ran through her mind day and night. Working harder to sort the company finances hadn't assuaged her guilt.

She, Stephanie, was the real coward.

She'd allowed Leah to think that taking over the reins of the fashion show and business had been an inconvenience, but the truth was that Stephanie revelled in it. She realised she'd been pushing Leah to success for her own reasons.

And now she was here in her sister's new world. With only a short text message from Leah in reply to her overtures through the private detective Stephanie had hired, she was nervous, worried left things too long. Left too much unsaid. There was so much ground to cover, so many misunderstandings. Flipping open her laptop she reread her speech to her sister, her explanation, excuses and regrets. It had taken days to compose.

She sighed. It was rubbish. It was too carefully crafted, too painstakingly perfected. Flipping the laptop closed, she looked across the ocean, lost in time.

Unconsciously, she clicked and unclicked her expensive pen – a habit she would not tolerate in others.

With thoughts loosely tangled, she doodled on the white napkin. The latte she had been so desperate for, was untouched. Then, with scarcely a bidden thought she wrote the words:

'I was wrong. Can you forgive me?'

A small hand reached for the napkin. Stephanie flinched and turned to grasp it back into her keeping, then hesitated. A familiar smile hovered above her.

'Leah? Oh, Leah ...'

Leah enjoyed Stephanie's visit but was keen to get back to her real life, the one she hadn't bothered to reveal to her sister, namely Adam Price and a fragile kid named Bridget.

Homemade

Adam arrived at midday and Leah picked Bridget up from school. The young girl had been staying over more often.

Leah revved the engine and wondered how to broach the subject of meeting Adam. 'Have you thought about…?

'I hope you know a good lawyer,' said Bridget, before clamming up on the subject.

'I do as it happens,' said Leah, knowing Adam wouldn't mind stretching the pasta he was making. 'My guy is a lawyer.'

'Oh, we're calling him "my guy" now. I see. There have been what the soap operas refer to as "developments".'

'Oh shut up, smarty-pants. You'll meet him at home. He's cooking.'

'Aha, that means no sandwiches or frozen meals then?'

'Okay, I know I can't cook.'

'I'm… maybe I should, um, go to my…'

'You're nervous. It's okay. If he hassles you, I'll give him time out.'

Bridget was ravenous.

'Keep that up, kid and you'll be as gorgeous as this one,' said Adam, wiping his hands on a flour covered apron.

'Oh, I ... Why are you covered in flour ... er ... Mr...'

'Call me Adam. It's m'name. I made the pasta. Messy business.'

'You cooked it from scratch? Wow, how'd you do that? It was so ... I thought it came in packets from ...'

'It's softer when you make it yourself,' said Adam. 'Stick around and I'll teach you sometime.'

'Oh, I couldn't ... you ...'

'I'd love to. I can't interest Ms Leah in my culinary adventures. She'd rather be off drawing dresses.'

'Designing clothes, thank you very much,' said Leah.

Adam rolled his eyes and Bridget giggled.

She'd never been in a home like this. Even with Ebony and her father there was sometimes tenseness in the air. Jenna said she was imagining things, but then Jenna had never had to live with the kind of fear Bridget had every day. It was hard to understand her friends sometimes. There was Ebony with a father bending over backwards to please her, and she was pushing him away; and Jenna spoke to her father as if he was, well, more like an overgrown brother. How could they ever understand?

She shifted in her seat, eyeing the clock.

'You have to be somewhere, kiddo?' asked Adam.

Leah was stacking the dishwasher. She was shocked at Adam's ease with Bridget and even more surprised by Bridget's response. Sensing that Bridget might open up to him,

197

Leah trundled outside with the rubbish bag.

'My dad will be furious. I should have been home and made tea hours ago. He'll be blind drunk by now ... and there'll be hell to pay.' Bridget pulled at the bandages on her hand.

'You're old enough to leave home, you know. Lots of kids do. There are better places than under leaky overturned boats, you know,' said Adam.

'How did you ...?'

'Leah.'

'You don't muck around when you have something to say, do you, Mr ... Adam?' Leah choked on the words.

'Life's too short, kid.'

'You don't understand. I can't just ...'

'He hits you, and God knows what else. You hate yourself for letting him. You're angry that your mother left you with him. But mostly, you're angry with yourself. How am I doing so far?'

Bridget sat open-mouthed, and then with her face reddening, she said, 'Okay, Sigmund Freud, great work. You've stated the problem. I guess you think that's halfway to some frigging where, but it doesn't solve anything.'

Adam handed Bridget a steaming cup of hot chocolate, then cradling his own mug, perched next to her on the bar stools.

'Heck, you don't waste time, do you? Now I understand how you swept Ms ... er, Leah ...' Bridget blushed.

Adam laughed. 'Yep, I know a good thing when I see it. So, what happened with your mum?'

Bridget sucked in a trembling breath and looked down. She grasped the mug with cramped fingers. She hesitated, drew a long breath, then her soft voice broke the silence.

'It's ... it's a bit ... like Ebony,' she sighed, wondering why it was easier to talk about someone else.

Adam waited.

'...well the worst thing is thinking your mother chose to leave you… That's what Eb went through...'

'Go on,' said Adam.

'It was ten years ago last term. I remember parts of it so well. It was my birthday. I was six ...' Bridget's voice cracked. 'mum used to work at the dry-cleaning place. I sometimes visited her there. We'd have a milkshake and chips. They were such good times together; I felt like the only ... kid in the world.' Bridget swiped awkwardly at a tear. 'She never said good-bye. She always sent cards but nothing this year. I hope nothing has happened to her. I plan to look for her when I'm older.'

'You have a brother, what's his name?'

Bridget snorted. 'Byron. He's getting rattier by the day. He smokes dope. I think he has a stash in the house. Anyway, he's only interested in escaping 'the hell hole'.'

'Your mum sounds lovely.' Adam titled his head.

'I've only got good memories, but they're kinda foggy. Now I hate the house and everything in it.'

Leah padded back into the room. 'You don't have to be there. We want to help. You don't have to have a five-year plan. We're offering you somewhere to figure things out.'

'Okay? If you hate us, you can tell us to shove off?' said Adam.

'I can tell *you to* ... oh funny; wouldn't I be the one shoving off? You live here.'

'I'm still working on that,' grinned Adam.

'Leah had all sorts of ways to escape but I'm a minor. I don't have rights, you know?'

'Bridget, you do have rights. A good many. You can get Living Away from Home Allowance from Centrelink and there are other things I'll go through with you. Leah have you got a writing pad?

Bridget looked at his crooked smile, the messy kitchen and the warm glow of the fire in the background and felt the sort of gratitude that expands your heart.

'Okay,' she said, and then because she couldn't think of anything else to say she added, 'your apron's undone.'

Investigation

'We can look up this Shirl at the same time.' Jenna settled into a chair at the library and had the electronic records in front of her in no time.

'Don't be dumb, Jenna. We're looking for Jean Galloway.' Ebony tried to share the chair.

'You're squashing me, Eb. Go find your own chair. Anyway, where's Bridget? Isn't she supposed to be here, helping us? We're doing this for her.'

'It's not easy for her, Jenna. I got really upset looking for Mum's records, anything that might give me hints. I wanted to find stuff, but I was afraid at the same time.' Ebony wiped a tear.

'Sorry, Eb. That must have been a horrid time for you. Wondering how your mum died. If it was suicide or…'

'Look what I found,' said Bridget, 'actual old fashioned paper newspapers.' She set them down on the table.

'Shit, Bridget, don't sneak up on us like that.' Jenna waved a cautionary hand.

'I came with you, Jenna. How is that sneaking?'

'Let's just get on with it. Ooh, newspapers. How far back to they go, Bridge?' asked Ebony.

Jenna pouted. 'We haven't got all day you two. I've only just been let out of the house since our nightclub disaster. Just because you two got off lightly.'

'Shut up, Jenna.' Ebony and Bridget said in unison.

Grey-mauve carpeting throughout the library muffled the sounds of a dozen lively conversations. There was a book club in the far corner where the glass windows joined at the side, allowing white strobes of light to vie with the angles of the tall metal artwork outside.

The girls found three computers side by side but Ebony and Bridget soon gravitated to Jenna, who was intensely quiet as she scrolled through Trove.

'There's no mention of any Galloways in any paper,' said Bridget, 'I belong to the most unremarkable family on the face of the earth.'

Ebony dragged a chair to Jenna's desk and Bridget soon followed.

'You'd think there would be a wedding notice at least,' said Jenna. 'Do you know your mother's maiden name, Bridge?'

'Nah. Maybe it was somewhere in the papers you photographed from the house.' Bridget swung her chair back and received a wagging finger from an observant librarian.

'Parents usually organised that, not the bride and groom. Did you ever meet your grandparents, Bridge?' asked Ebony.

'I don't remember,' Bridget chewed her lip. 'Adam told me

that people like my father are experts at driving family and friends away, like they never existed. And for kids there are no memories.'

'Gosh, I'd miss my Grandie and Nan and Nonna. That must be awful.' Ebony squished in to try and see the screen better.

'Don't crowd me Eb. Who's Nonna?'

'Iris. Emma's mother. The hairdresser. She's lovely.'

'So I work for your grandmother?' said Bridget. 'Ha, what do you know.'

'Shush. There's something here about young Tom Galloway wood chopping at the show. "A fine demonstration of speed and tenacity from young Tom Galloway" and a photo.'

Bridget and Ebony stared, while Jenna counted on her fingers.

'What are you doing Jenna?'

'I just worked out that your father is 62 years old.'

Bridget sat open-mouthed. 'So he doesn't just look old. He is old,' she whispered. 'Really old.'

'Really, really old,' said Jenna.

'Crikey, he's about the same age as Grandie.' Ebony stretched and massaged her neck. 'Let's take a break and come back. Then we can look at the photos you took, Jenna.'

Jenna jumped up as if Ebony has just cracked the enigma code. 'We'll all get flash-drives so we have backup of the photos. That way it will be impossible for things to get lost.'

The girls got ice-creams and flash-drives. Too antsy to walk around, Jenna suggested they go back to the library as soon as they'd finished the ice-creams. With the newspapers delivering so little information she couldn't wait to look at the photos on a large screen.

'We can print stuff out if we want to.'

It was torture for Bridget. She'd looked forward to having a better view, but the more images that flicked onto the screen the more aware she became that there were no photos of her or Byron. She felt like a large hand had reached into her chest and was crushing her heart.

She looked away. It was too much. 'I'm gonna go.'

Ebony hugged her. 'I get it. Are you gonna faint? Can I get you a drink?'

Bridget was taken aback by the affectionate gesture. She couldn't remember the last time she'd been hugged. Byron rubbed his knuckles on her head and gave brief hugs, but the genuine empathy from a friend who had gone through hell over her own mother, was unfamiliar and unexpectedly moving.

Jenna made three copies of the flash drive, and then they tapped the drives together and said, 'one for all and all for one'.

Jenna stayed and watched the other two walk out of the library. It was too soon to give up. She flicked the cards that Bridget had received from her mother and compared the writing to the writing on the accounts by Horsey Carol. She was shocked at similarity of the script. Had Horsey Carol written the cards? Was she the one who'd slipped then into Bridget's drawer? That would explain Bridget's father's anger when he found out. It had always seemed odd to Jenna that Tom Galloway would veto any mention of Bridget's mother and then give out cards and letters from her.

But the thought that someone else had written the letters opened up a whole new train of thought that was totally confusing. Who was Horsey Carol? If she had written and delivered them, what did that mean?

Jenna was pleased to see Byron pacing in the park. He'd have to have some useful piece of information.

'Hey Byron.' Jenna ran towards him.

'Oh shit,' said Byron when he saw the leggy blonde coming towards him. He could take off but it would be no use. That girl was so fit she could outrun anything. Probably did track and field. And she was like a dog with a bone.

'Did you get cards from your mum?' asked Jenna, still running on the spot.

'What the fuck? What are you on?'

'Did you?'

'I s'pose.'

'Have you still got them?'

'Fucked if I know.'

'Think, Byron, think.'

But all that Byron could think was that he didn't need this bossy cow messing up his plans. He wasn't in the park to go down the slippery slide. The thought made him smile.

'You should do that more often,' said Jenna.

'What?' Byron had lost not only his train of thought but the direction of the conversation Jenna was trying to navigate with him.

'Smile,' said Jenna, 'especially while you still have your

teeth, before they rot and fall out because of all the shit you're shoving in your face.'

Byron opened his mouth to respond in a fitting manner and get Jenna to leave him alone but she'd already gone, loping along with that ponytail swinging like a helicopter rotor.

He felt his teeth. He was fond of his teeth.

Business

Byron had been in the middle of some very difficult calculations when Jenna had accosted him. He was negotiating the price of the stash he had hidden in his old man's house. Benji had set the whole thing up. The offer to step up to dealing had been too good to refuse. Now that he'd lost his job. Fancy that hypocrite Dave sacking him when the guy used the stuff himself.

It was easy to store the bags of hash at his father's house. The old bloke hardly moved from the sofa. He hadn't blinked when Byron had started to visit more often. The old dude was too self-absorbed to look past his own needs and had taken to asking Byron to run around after him on his short visits home. No wonder Bridget had legged it out on the first opportunity.

Where was Benji? He shuddered as he saw a movement in the shrubs. He was dying for a spliff to calm his nerves. All he wanted to do was hand Benji's buyer a sample of the gear, sell it, then and get the hell out of there. He hoped Benji wouldn't take long checking the stuff out because he wanted to shift it from the house as soon as he could. His old man was losing control after Bridget had moved in with that uptown woman and her solicitor boyfriend. He'd taken to abusing neighbours and the number of debt collectors was increasing.

It was only a matter of time before the cops called around to warn him. Byron couldn't afford for them to stumble on the bags and the cash. He'd have to find somewhere else to set up. If this deal went off, he'd be able to rent a small place and keep a low profile.

But this was a one-off. There was no way he was going through this kind of anxiety again. Hanging out in parks in daylight.

Benji was expecting the buyer to take the whole stash but Byron was having none of that. He had only bought a sample, a generous one, but not the whole amount. That's how his previous dealer had done things and it made sense. Benji took too many chances. Byron rubbed his hands together, thinking of the money. A bloody decent sum if it all went through.

Everything would be different after tonight.

When Benji finally showed up he was as nervous as hell. Usually the one to laugh at Byron's tendency to worry, he was jittery. Looking left and right, right and left.

'Where's the buyer, Benji?' he asked.

'Where's the stash, Byron? Have ya brought it?'

'Nah. I'm not working that way. Too risky, mate. So where's the buyer. I've got a sample. That's all.'

The buyer sauntered over as if he was just buying a Mars bar. Cool customer. The sample was brought out, sold.

Someone from the shadows and the "buyer" brought out handcuffs and arrested them both. Byron watched Benji moan about the cuffs and swearing at the cops, and knew he'd been right not to trust Benji. Too late. Shit. That sample was enough to get him in a lot of trouble. Serving time was on the table.

Everything would be different after tonight.

Search

The hall clock chimed the hour.

Jim Harcourt interrupted his granddaughter. 'Hold that thought, kiddo. I have to check on your Nan.'

Ebony was left gaping into the silence, forming sentences for Grandie, but when he returned his face was ashen. He headed straight for the phone.

'Brady, I need you,' he said. 'Your mother's gone missing.'

Within minutes Brady ran through the open door and embraced his father.

Tears flowed down Jim's face. 'It's my fault, Son.'

'No, it's not. It's going to be all right, Dad. We'll find her. Where's Misty?'

'Oh, I never thought to check.'

Brady sent Ebony to look around the house for the Labrador that never left his mother's side, while he phoned the police.

'Betty Harcourt ... she's frail ... 'How long has she been

gone, Dad?'... Dad doesn't know, she was in bed two hours ago ... she's in her eighties ... Alzheimer's ... yes ... no, I don't think there are medication issues for tonight ... Dad, what was she wearing' ...?'

Jim Harcourt stood and took the phone. 'She went in her dressing gown and slippers. They aren't by the bed where she leaves them ... pale blue ... She must have gone out the front door. I was talking with my granddaughter in the kitchen by the back door .... She has a dog with her, a Labrador ... yes, very protective, he won't leave her side ... No, she doesn't need medication tonight, but she will in the morning ... mild blood pressure ... it's so cold, please Constable ...' Jim broke down. 'I should have been paying more attention. I must have left the key in the door. I usually...' Wordlessly he handed Brady the phone. After a few brisk sentences, Brady hung up.

'Can I do something, Dad?' asked Ebony.

'...yes,' he said, 'stay here. If Nan comes home ring us straight away. And keep her here.'

'Can I phone Jenna to stay with me? Jack will want to help.'

'Yes. Good, we need all the manpower we can get. Where's that floodlight torch of yours Dad?'

'She can't have gone far,' said Jim.

'Don't worry, Dad. I'm here now.'

Brady went to the coat stand by the door and pulled Jim's moleskin jacket off the hook. He gently helped his father into it. 'It's going to be okay, Dad.'

The next few minutes were a flurry of activity. Jack Bragg arrived with Jenna who went straight to Ebony and hugged her. Then they huddled together on the two seater lounge in the dining room as if they themselves were also lost.

The cops didn't take long.

Sergeant Peter Benson had only recently arrived for his new posting in Noarlunga, and he viewed this fact as an advantage. This opinion was not shared by many of the other police officers and Sgt. Peter Benson was well aware of those who saw his position in a poor light. Some were officers who had nurtured hopes of taking the job on and others simply didn't like change. Then there were the garden variety whingers who were just born disagreeable. Many thought him smug and distant. He knew he was the subject of speculation.

Peter Benson cared for none of this. The longer they tried to figure him out, the more time he had to find the lay of the land. They may have heard he'd been previously involved in officer training and right him off as out of touch. That was just fine. What they wouldn't have known was his experience and training in psychology. He was well aware that he lacked 'local knowledge', but arriving fresh from the western suburbs of Sydney gave him something else—objectivity.

Two of his officers had done a drug bust earlier and one of the arrested guys was shaking and whimpering and the other was yelling in his sleep, then complaining about having nightmares about his teeth. 'That's Galloway,' said one of the officers, 'bad as his father. Drunk as a skunk and driving us mad with his yodelling. Teeth, for goodness sakes. Couldn't he be more creative than teeth?'

The men laughed.

In the cell, Byron cringed. So that's what they thought? What had happened to the charming salesman with slick clothes, and respect? Respect was over. He'd never been called Galloway. That had been reserved for his father. And now he was exactly where his father had been. Hospital, then the lock up. Great.

'Have they been drug tested? Evaluated?' asked Sergeant Peter Benson. 'Had a chance for a phone call?'

'Galloway reckons there's no one to phone. Said he's been sacked, and we all know his father, trouble that one.

Sergeant Peter Benson didn't take the call about the missing woman, but his senses were on alert as soon as the phone rang. He casually strolled into the reception area where a junior officer was answering the call. Grateful that the young policeman on duty with him was a local, he saw the night shift as a perfect opportunity to glean information. And young Darren Clamont was perfect. A good natured kid who was often reproached by the older officers for running off at the mouth, Darren would prove a useful companion and Peter Benson intended to make full use of the long night.

'It's a missing woman, Serg, an elderly one,' Damien said, covering the mouthpiece. 'Do you want to take the call?'

'No constable, not yet. Get a good description, any health issues ... I'll talk to them when you have some details.'

Damien beamed. 'Yes, Sir ... er thanks ...'

Benson smiled at the young man's gratitude. No one else called him Sir, but Benson didn't correct him. By the time he took the phone from Damien he'd gleaned most of the facts. He was particularly adept at working out one-sided conversations. He'd had to be in his undercover days. A life might hang in the balance then, usually his.

He allowed the younger man to drive. There was no time to waste. The old woman had Alzheimer's and couldn't be counted on to find her way home with any ease. At least she had been wearing a thick dressing gown and footwear. This would spare her from the night's winter chill to a degree. She also had a companion dog with her. The situation was of concern, but there were many things in their favour.

It was only a twenty minute drive to the home of the Harcourts. It was a fruitful twenty minutes. By the time they'd arrived at the house, Benson knew a lot more than the initial details taken at the station. Jim Harcourt was the sole carer for his wife. He was in denial about the full extent of his wife's condition. He'd been struggling for some time, refusing many offers of help from his friends. Jim had been a very active member of the community before his wife's total dependence on him, so the support systems he had brushed aside would be considerable. There was a son living nearby.

'Did you speak to the son?' asked Peter.

'Yes, he took over from the husband. Poor old Jim was shattered, blames himself for his wife wandering off. The son is a competent sort of bloke, manages the polyclinic.'

Sergeant Benson was out of the car, already shaking the hand of a tall man holding the door open. He saw the raw anxiety in the man's face.

'Thanks, for coming...'

'Sergeant Peter Benson, and you must be the son.'

'Yes,' said Brady. 'I'm Brady Harcourt.'

'So what's happening, Brady?'

A quick exchange of facts told the sergeant that Brady had a good deal of common sense. He had his daughter and a neighbour woman sitting with his father, who he had side-tracked from searching too far by recommending that he search the house thoroughly.

'I have a survey of the estate and its surroundings,' said Brady.

'Gosh, you are organised,' said Benson, taking the proffered pages. 'This will be most useful.'

The sergeant swung into operational mode. Flicking on his high-powered torch he asked for more details, then gave instructions to them all. Jim Harcourt had joined the group, and Sergeant Benson quickly surmised that the man was fit to be part of the search and in fact would be helpful. After all, he had the best knowledge of the property and the wife. Jack Bragg, a private investigator, arrived and Emma Harcourt, Brady's wife.

'Form a chain, stay in sight of each other and fan out. Has everyone got a torch? I'll be in the middle of the line and Constable Clamont will take the end near the heaviest bushland. Thank goodness it's a full moon, that will help visibility. Call out to her, especially you, Jim. What we're looking at here is a woman who doesn't want to be lost and that will work for us. Let's get moving. Betty will be getting cold, that's our biggest worry.'

The full rising moon gave long shadows to the sullen greys of the bush. The air was chilled and getting colder. Benson kept an eye on the searchers as well as for any signs of the woman. They couldn't afford a break in the line. No one spoke, other than to call for Betty, their voices leaden and anxious.

Jim Harcourt's eyes were focused and determined. His stride was strong and purposeful. Benson had deliberately put the older man next to him in the search. He wanted to observe him. There were inevitable questions that required answers. Being an outsider gave Benson a detached view that some might have assessed as cynical. Disappearances of loved ones was usually straightforward, and this case had all the overtones of there being no hidden agenda, but instincts honed over decades in the force told him that things weren't always as they seemed. The old man had allowed himself to become isolated with his wife. There were huge frustrations in being a sole carer. Jim's angst seemed genuine, but Sgt. Peter Benson would withhold judgement. He'd look at every angle.

Half an hour passed. The group had thoroughly searched the estate land. The fence was down in many places, laying in a tangled, rusty heap. There was a hush as they realised Betty must have wandered onto the Galloway property. The area of bushland was larger and more secluded than Peter had first thought. Maps were deceiving. On instinct he chose a gap with a clearer passage in the fence and beamed his high powered torch in the area. Calling the group together he said, 'She must have crossed the fenceline.'

'The Galloway property is at least ten acres,' said Constable Darren Clamont. 'It will take hours ... hey Serg, here's a slipper.' He handed the slipper to Jim.

'That's Betty's,' said Jim, panic flashing across his face.

'Through here, people, and fan out. Keep it slow and careful.'

Benson said nothing as they crossed into the Galloway property. He kept the young constable by his side and let the others go ahead. 'Tell me about the Galloways, Constable. We're on their land now and things could get tricky, although we have every right in an emergency.'

'Oh, okay,' said the constable.

Darren had plenty to say. Benson smiled in the dark. This kid was Google on legs.

'Old Galloway, the father's a raving drunk, plastered by lunchtime. Yells blue murder at anyone who goes near the place. The son's a junkie. Byron, sells mobile phones. Bad sort. We've been trying to nail him for dealing. He's been a slippery bastard, but we finally got him. He's in the cells at the station now. There's a daughter. Teenager. A Goth kid, Bridget. Sad story that one. She gets a raw deal. Sorry, Serg, I'm rambling. The others tell me to leave off the gossip ... but I grew up here...'

'Don't you listen to them, Constable. You're doing fine. It's all good intel.' The sergeant tapped the side of his head. 'Where does this Byron live?'

'He lives with the old man, I think. I dunno. Well, he's there often enough although there's no love lost. The old bloke's an angry cuss of wasted breath. We used to be called out there every other Friday night for a domestic before the wife up and left. Actually we have Galloway's son in custody for drugs. Enough to charge him.'

'Hmm.' Benson committed all these snippets to memory. It would make for some interesting reading back at the station.

'The old bloke owns at least a dozen acres. But there's a hell of a chunk of bushland right down to the Galloway place.

That's one rundown joint. I can't see the old girl, sorry, Mrs Harcourt, gettin' that far, anyway that barbed wire fencing—she wouldn't manage that by all reckoning.'

'People do some amazing things when they're mentally impaired, but physically okay. How's her mobility.'

'Oh, right. Yeah, she's pretty good on her pins.'

Another ten minutes passed. The bush was dense and progress slow. Jim's voice grew plaintive, 'Misty, where are you boy? Where's Betty, mate?'

Peter's trained ear heard a faint canine whimper and shone his torch in the direction of the sound. Jim called louder, 'Misty?'

The dog began to bark and leapt towards Jim. Peter swept the arc of light. There was a pink bundle near an old tree stump. Betty Harcourt was sound asleep.

'Oh my God, Betty. Are you alright?' Jim Harcourt sobbed as he lifted the old woman to her feet and swung her up into his arms. 'This will never happen again, Betty. I promise.'

Benson signalled that the search was over. He turned on his heel towards the young constable. There was something he wanted to check, and he needed to do it alone. Something had caught his eye out there. Something that triggered a gut instinct. Just a flash, but experience told him to check. He wouldn't get another chance. He'd need a search warrant next time. Calmly instructing Clamont to take notes, he strode back into the brush. He gave no explanation. Life had taught him that playing his cards close to his chest got the best results. The constable didn't hesitate, pleased to be given responsibility. There wasn't a real necessity for taking more notes, but he knew Darren would not question his actions and that would buy him some time.

With unerring footsteps, Peter Benson went straight to the object that had caught his eye. It was a man's red and black flannelette shirt. A totally ordinary garment, aged by years in the bush, probably accidently discarded, then forgotten, nothing that would arouse suspicion in most men, but Peter Benson wasn't most men. The place was about 10 metres further than they'd found Betty.

He slipped gloves on with the ease of years of experience and slipped the shirt into a plastic evidence bag. Shining the torch at the nearby surroundings he saw a huge curved tree stump a good fifty metres further on, where there were signs of recent human presence. He was sure no-one else had noticed anything. Walking towards the tree stump he noticed a discarded cigarette paper and the lid of a beer bottle.

He'd bet good money this was someone's secret place. Someone careful enough to take the bottle they'd been drinking and leave nothing else but a small discarded cigarette butt of the roll-your-own-kind. Slipping the butt into another bag, Benson turned to join the others. He made a mental note to return in daylight.

He stuffed the shirt under his jacket. An ordinary find? Maybe. But that rusty stain on the shirt aroused all of Sergeant Peter Benson's red flags. He didn't like an unsolved mystery and if he had to DNA test everyone who'd ever walked across that area, he would.

Missing Person

Constable Darren Clamont was on the front desk of the police station when Bridget sidled in the front door with her hoodie pulled over her face for her appointed interview. Darren knew her, or of her, to be more precise. Bridget always wore long sleeves and clutched at her wrists when she was anxious. He hoped she hadn't followed her brother's example, although they hadn't turned up anything but marijuana in Byron's tests.

'I'm glad you came in kiddo,' he said. 'I'll just get Constable Strong, she'll look after you.' Picking up the intercom he spoke briefly, 'Jessica, can I have your assistance at the desk, please.' Turning back to Bridget he said, 'She'll be right out.'

'... er, okay.' Hands thrust in her pockets, Bridget didn't move.

Darren kept talking while they waited. He didn't want Bridget to leave. She looked as if she'd slept on the street. Her dark smudged eyes were heavy-lidded with fear, and something else; there was a wraith of hopelessness around her.

A young woman entered the waiting area. 'Hello, Bridget. Do you mind coming through with me?'

Bridget noticed INTERVIEW ROOM on the door they entered.

'Take a seat, Bridget. I'm Constable Jessica Strong. Thanks for coming in. Would you like a coffee?' Without waiting for an answer, the officer called out, 'Get us a couple of coffees, would you Darren? And go light on the sugar, we don't want to thicken up round the middle like you.'

Bridget sat on a hard backed chair. A shy smile teased the corner of her mouth, but it failed to erase the tension on her face. 'Why do you want to see me?'

'It's about your mother, Bridget. We've opened a Missing Persons' case on her.'

'Oh, right. Mr Wainwright said.'

'She went missing; what, ten years ago? What do you remember of her?'

'Not missing exactly. She ran off ...' Her eyes clouded. '... on my sixth birthday. I dunno.'

'That must have been hard.'

Bridget grasped the mug with cramped fingers. '...well the worst thing is thinking that your mother chose to leave you.' Bridget sucked in a trembling breath and looked down.

'Go on,' said Jessica. Her fist clenched under the table. There was a dark bruise on Bridget's neck.

'I remember parts of it really well. Mum said it was going to be a special birthday; things were gonna change, you know?' Bridget's voice cracked. 'She was acting differently, as if she had a secret. I thought it was because she was planning my party.'

'How did she seem? Was she happy?'

'She was kind of excited. She said things were gonna to be different. I didn't know what she meant. I guess she was planning to leave. Da said she ran off with a sales rep from her job at the dry cleaners. I sometimes visited her there. They were good times together ...' Bridget swiped awkwardly at a tear. 'She never said good-bye.'

'She sounds lovely.'

'How lovely could she be!? Who walks out on their kids and only sends cards? Even those stopped a couple of years ago. Who just gets up and leaves their kids?'

'Do you know that for sure?'

'Well ... I guess she might have, she, I dunno ... Da wouldn't have told us. He would have warned her off, or ...'

'...or what Bridget?' Did your parents get along?'

Bridget looked up and blinked. 'Da yelled a lot. Still does. He gets really angry if things aren't done right. Friday nights were the worst ... He'd get fully drunk after work. When he had a job, that is.'

There was silence in the room as Constable Strong scribbled quick notes. Bridget wanted to ask if she could go, if they were done, but she didn't want to disturb the officer.

Another policeman entered the room. He was tall and straight. His uniform stretched across his shoulders as he moved. He had a different aura to the other officers. Something steely and determined. His features were rounded and generous, belying his impressive demeanour. Sergeant

Peter Benson brought a folder and handed it to the female officer. The room grew cold and dark. The sounds of the papers being shuffled were loud, fragmented. Shards of pain shattered in Bridget's head.

Sergeant Benson sat down and Constable Strong leaned back in the chair. Another officer arrived with a tray of steaming coffees.

'Bridget, I'm Sergeant Peter Benson. How are you doing?'

'I've got the creeps.'

'Of course you do. Nasty bit of business, and then us, subjecting you to this kind of thing. But it seems as though this process should have happened years ago. Thank so much for helping. We're grateful.'

Bridget gulped the coffee, relieved she hadn't been called in to for an interview regarding the night of the nightclub drama. A night where she could remember so little, and yet enough. Enough for her to cut her hair, throw out her black makeup and never, ever forget that she'd been called low hanging fruit and then treated like garbage. If it hadn't been for Leah. Leah standing up for her. For her own choice, her own right to reveal or not. To go to the police or not. Leah hadn't told anyone. She might be the first person Bridget had trusted in an age.

'Bridget,' Sergeant Benson began, 'are you aware that we are now treating your mother's disappearance as a Missing Person case. This was not something that we undertook previously because it was assumed that your mother left voluntarily. Sadly, the matter was not investigated. Your father's explanation was accepted at face value. But we have a different view now. A shirt was found. In the bush on your father's property. There is a blood stain.' Benson spoke slowly, carefully. Giving the facts piecemeal so the girl could take it all in.

Bridget began to shake. The room spun. She sucked air in hungrily. But she mustn't lose control. Mustn't faint. This was too important. Placing both hands firmly on the table she looked the sergeant in the eye.

'So you think that blood might be my mother's?' Bridget gripped the table.

'We want to rule that possibility out, or in. Yes, we think that it's a possibility. Your mother never collected her last wages and our earlier conversations with her employer, Mrs Wainwright, confirmed our suspicions that your mother had not intended to run away with anyone.'

'But ... we've, I've gotten cards from Mum, a letter or two even. She can't be dead.'

'I know this is hard, Bridget. We don't know, that's why this is called an investigation. Can you be absolutely certain that it was your mother's handwriting on those cards and letters?'

'I, well...' Bridget slumped. 'I was only six, but Da... Oh God ... how could I believe anything he says.'

Sergeant Benson placed a sheet of paper in front of Bridget. 'Bridget, we would like you to let us take a sample of your saliva and blood for a DNA test.

'DNA?' she said.

'I'll give it straight to you, Bridget. We're testing DNA on the shirt.' He placed a hand on the sheet of paper. 'Don't jump to any conclusions, Bridget. These are just procedures we have to go through. We've not identified any of the DNA yet. At sixteen you can waive your right to have a parent or carer present. Only if you are okay to do so.'

'Sure. I'm find with that. It's just a lot to take in. Mum could be dead, or maybe Da cut himself chopping down a tree. Or someone else left the shirt there.'

'Yes, Bridget. All those things are possible.'

Bridget sipped her tea as the room stopped spinning and her breathing returned to normal. Her mother had been gone ten years. She spent her birthdays and free time at the cemetery. As Jenna had said, how much worse can the truth be?'

Bridget fudged a smile. 'Will it tell if Da is my real father?'

'He wouldn't give us his DNA. Are you worried about that?'

Bridget shrugged. 'I'd rather anyone else on earth was my father.'

A curious man

The old weatherboard house drooped in despair. The sheer burden of existence had sunk the foundation stumps unevenly. The paint had peeled in sheets. Dark rotting boards had simply given up and crumbled, giving the house gave a stench that spoke of something greater than simple neglect.

There were areas where someone had made a token effort. A cluster of daisies struggled for life beside the tilted front veranda, their yellow glory diminished by the overwhelming decline of the house. A feeble cough of smoke escaped from the chimney, suggesting the presence of life.

Two policemen approached what appeared to be the front entrance, and paused. Clearly the leader, one of them was tall, with the lithe grace of an athlete. His uniform was stretched across broad shoulders. He walked a little behind the younger officer, who was picking his way through discarded carcasses of cars with ease. He'd been there before.

A shadow flashed at a window in the closed-in veranda.

The tall policeman knocked loudly at the door.

A sound came from inside the house, a tinkle of breaking glass, then silence.

The officer pounded again.

Tom Galloway was in the front room, but he intended to wait it out. There was no way he was answering the door. The cops came around a fair bit. And left.

The men stepped to the side, away from the door. They stood near the sunroom window. Tom strained to hear their mumbled voices. One of them was young Darren Clamont. The other man spoke, a low burr he couldn't make out, he seemed to pose a question.

'What are you mongrels doin' sneakin' around my property? That you, Darren? And who are you, tough guy? Don't put ya hands on me ... I'll have ya. See if I don't.'

Tom Galloway opened the door a crack, assuming he still had the safety of the darkened screen door, but it was wide open, and swift advantage was taken by Sergeant Peter Benson who thrust a heavy boot in the doorway.

It should have taken less time for Tom Galloway to work out that Sergeant Peter Benson was made of sterner stuff than he was accustomed to. When confronted with the news that he was being taken in for questioning Tom Galloway acquiesced, under protest. With chin in the air, he pouted all the way to the station in the back of the car.

At the police station, Sergeant Benson simply waited until Galloway ran out of steam, out of swear words, out of rants and ravings, while he calmly perused a large file. With Tom Galloway's name on it.

'Well, are you gonna to tell me?' Galloway growled.

Benson took a moment. 'Tell you what, Tom?'

'Why I'm here. I aint done nothing.'

'I'm a curious man, Mr Galloway. A curious man.' Benson flicked the intercom. 'Can you bring Mr Galloway some sandwiches, Darren? What's your choice, Tom? Never mind. We've only got BLT.'

'I dunno what BLT is.' Tom Galloway nodded. He was hungry. He might as well have something to eat. Lunch on the cops, why not. If only he could make sense of the bloke in front of him. One minute he was calling him Tom, the next Mr. Galloway. Gave a man the shivers. Taking his time like that.

While Galloway wolfed down the sandwiches, Benson spoke, slowly and clearly.

'We found an interesting item on your property, Mr Galloway. A red shirt. He flicked the intercom again. 'Constable, can you bring that flannelette shirt in here.'

Constable Clamont brought in a plastic bag with a shirt. The bag was designated with the words EVIDENCE.

Tom gulped at those words, barely looking at the shirt.

'I dunno. How'd I remember me clobber, hardly remember from one day to the next. Although it's nice for you fellas to take an interest in a man's wardrobe.'

Tom's bravado evaporated at the Sergeant's next statement.

'We found blood on the shirt.'

'A man cuts himself all the time.'

'So you're saying that this shirt is yours?'

'No, I'm bloody not. Don't recognise it.'

'There was enough blood on the shirt to send off for DNA, along with other fibres.'

'Ha, what's the use of results? You aint got my DNA and you aint gettin' it. So, you can just leave a man in peace and let me go home.'

'You're correct Mr Galloway. We don't have your DNA. However we have your daughter's DNA. And it matches the male DNA on the shirt, meaning that a relative of hers owns the shirt. However, the blood is another story. It is from an unknown female, a young female.' Benson paused, realising Galloway's cognitive function might be impaired by alcohol. But when wasn't it?

Galloway stopped mid-chew and narrowed his eyes.

'How dare you approach my daughter without my permission? She's a minor. You aint got nothin'.'

'Your daughter is sixteen. She's old enough for a good many things, Mr Galloway. She can leave home. Choose to live where she wishes. And take out an AVO on the father who has been using physical violence to control her. Here is the paperwork for **that**. As you can see it is marked ex-parte, which means that the magistrate did not require your presence. These conditions apply even if Bridget returns to live in your home, although she has chosen not to do so at this time. However, if she does, you won't just be a brutal bully, you will be breaking the law if you lay a hand on her and it will be my personal pleasure to arrest and charge you.'

Tom Galloway reddened, hands clenched into fists.

'Have you understood what I've told you, Mr Galloway, or

would you like me to repeat it from the beginning?'

Mr Tom Galloway found that particular prospect so unappealing that, in spite of not comprehending the whole, he grabbed the paperwork and declared loudly he was ready to leave.

The officers drew straws as to who would drive the angry old bastard home. Constable Clamont lost, and was quite convinced the others had cheated, considering the number of times this circumstance landed him on the wrong end of the procedure.

When Tom Galloway arrived home the house was silent. Bridget's room was neat, spare, empty. The rage he was unable to take out on his daughter was turned into the mother of all binges. When Carol, the horsey woman arrived he threw a beer bottle at her, hitting her in the head. Carol, whose long-suffering company had been Galloway's only comfort in life, was forced to attend the A&E where the staff were privy to a loud and aggrieved account of the incident. 'And I don't care who knows'. This tirade continued until an offer to call the police turned her rantings to murmurings, but did not diminish her sense of mistreatment. Enough was enough.

The head nurse, free of the imposition of breaking confidences due to Carol's public ranting told Sergeant Peter Benson of the incident over afternoon tea.

Benson, already creating a list of lines of investigations, added Carol and the incident to his list.

He clutched the pencil so tightly that it broke. How he longed to get a dozen officers out to Tom Galloway's scrubland and go over it with a fine tooth comb.

However, he didn't have enough evidence and the old bloke was never going to give permission.

And that was when fate smiled on Sergeant Peter Benson.

A 000 call notified that smoke was billowing from the Galloway property.

This news galvanised Benson who had little interest in any fire, but a great deal of interest in the Galloway scrub.

The officers in his command didn't question when he requested the forensic team's attendance.

Fire

Leah answered an insistent bashing on her front door.

Ebony and Jenna tumbled in.

'There's a fire, Bridge. Seems to be at your place,' Jenna said, leaving polite introductions in the dust.

'What?' Bridget dropped her toast.

Outside the cottage, smoke billowed over the nearby houses.

Bridget ran.

She cleared the grevilleas.

The house was gone, a smouldering, flatbed of rubble, less than the bonfire had been a decade ago.

There were sleek red firetrucks, police cars, an ambulance.

Half a dozen firies with their face shields pressed back were gathered on the uneven paved area at the back of the house. Bridget heard snatches of their conversation.

'…rundown old place…'

'...went up like tinder...'

'...spread to the scrub before we got here...'

'...Galloway ... lousy, wife-beating drunk...'

'...missus cleared out years ago...'

'...silly old bloke smoking in bed...'

'...old dump, waste of our time...'

'...what's that sweet skunk smell?...'

'...was the old bloke smoking Mary Jane?...'

'...someone was, helluva stink...'

Several police officers headed out of the bushland in the neighbouring paddock. They carried a black body bag. An officer with them had clear plastic bags with red-lettered words— EVIDENCE.

Bridget dropped to her knees. Had Da been caught in the fire? Had he tried to run from the fire into the scrub? Then she heard his voice, howling like an animal. There was activity near the ambulance. And more policemen.

She tried to stand but couldn't.

Where was Byron?

What was happening? Her body jerked and shuddered out of control. She clutched her backpack so hard she heard the metal of her art tin inside the bag screech.

A scream pierced the chilled air. Bridget touched her throat. Was that her? A police officer saw, or heard her. She didn't know which.

'The daughter's okay,' he yelled. 'She can't have been in the house.'

'Thank God for small mercies,' said voice. It belonged to an orange-suited paramedic, heading her way, a small blonde woman with kind eyes.

The paramedic took her blood pressure. Calm reassuring words fluttered in the air. Bridget swallowed grateful sips of water as the paramedic sat her upright.

Over by the police cars the body bag was on the ground. Police stood around it chatting. One of the younger cops walked over to the paramedic with Bridget. He carried evidence bags.

'It's your lucky day, kiddo. Just as well you weren't here,' he said to Bridget, and received a sharp elbow jab from the paramedic.

'Naff off idiot,' said the paramedic. 'Take those away.' She pointed at the bags and jerked her head towards the police standing around the body bag. 'Frigging novice.'

'Don't be like that, Constable.' The young cop pouted with exaggerated offense. As he turned to leave Bridget's eyes fixed on the clear plastic bags he held.

One contained fabric, a garment? It was muddy, torn and covered in leaves. Stained dark iron-red. It looked knitted, fluffy.

It was the palest blue she'd ever seen.

Her mother's favourite shawl. Wrapped around Bridget the night before their mother left.

Bridget went down like a rock just as Jenna, Ebony and Leah arrived, followed by Brady and some other men.

Benson's list

Earl Wainwright was the first person on Benson's list. Benson found Earl to be forthright yet astute on the phone and they agreed to meet at the Old Noarlunga Hotel for a meal and a chat.

'You have a healthy appetite for a trim sort of bloke,' said Benson as they finished their meals and ordered a beer.

'Yes, it always nettled Prue,' said Earl. 'Now, I take it as good news that you wanted to chat off duty.' Earl smiled as he wiped his face with a serviette.

'Earl, I want to thank you for setting up a missing person's report for Jean Galloway. We're putting resources into that. It's worrying, and I'll be straight with you. I'm concerned about Bridget Galloway living with that brute, Tom.'

'I can relieve your mind on that score, Peter. She's moved in with the new woman, the fashion designer. They've had similar experiences and they've become close.' Earl leaned the chair back and stretched his long legs. 'So Bridget lives near her friends in Brighton Court, a cul-de-sac a few kilometres from the old man. He's always been a brute. When we were young bucks he was the loudest, raunchiest bloke in any pub, the first to hone in on the youngest sheila.'

'He's an itch I can't scratch, Earl. There's something but I can't put a finger on it. Keeps me awake. Our search warrant wasn't much use when the house had burned to ash. Of course, you know we found a body in the scrub, still some searching to do yet. It doesn't seem feasible that Jean Galloway ran off with some bloke.'

'Prue had a similar feeling. It worried her right up till she died. She was talking about Jean. How she never believed Jean ran off with a bloke. They were close. Jean and Prue. Prue was a tough woman in her working life, never got close to colleagues. But it was different with Jean. Prue made a bit of a fuss in the early days. Saying there should be a missing person's report.'

'There's no record of her doing that,' said Peter, wrinkling his forehead. 'Damn it.'

'I can tell you what she said, if it's any use.' Earl summoned a waitress and ordered an Irish Coffee.

'I'll have the same,' said Peter, 'and I'd love to hear your version.'

'Well, Tom vowed black and blue that Jean didn't come home on the Thursday, but Prue saw her outside the Galloway house on Friday morning, in her uniform, probably waiting for a taxi because the buses were on strike. Jean was waiting by the side of the road with a warm coat and her favourite shawl. Prue sent our driver back to get her, but he was gone for ages, with no excuse so Prue sacked him.'

'That shawl. We found a pale blue shawl in the scrubland at Galloways with a bloodstain.'

'No wonder it's keeping you awake at night, Peter. I assume you've sent it for DNA and are waiting.'

'Naturally. We'll know more when that comes back.'

'And the body you found?' asked Earl. 'You think it's Jean? Or maybe not?'

'You're an astute man, Earl. No, I don't. Jean was tall and this body is of a shorter woman. And initial investigations indicate it has been there longer than ten years. The DNA on the shirt doesn't match anyone. I'm trying to get as much background on Galloway as I can. So far Bridget is the only one co-operating, but she was only six ... but she swears the blue bloodstained shawl was her mother's, says Jean wrapped her in it every night, so we have to keep searching. Jean must be there, in there somewhere. There's a decent amount of blood on the shawl. We know Galloway has owned and lived on the property for the past forty years. So it's not a lot of point checking previous owners. The DNA should provide answers.'

The waitress arrived with their coffees. They sat in silence, sipping the soothing liquid.

Earl broke the silence. 'There are a few of the old gang that hung out here in the old days. The hairdresser, Iris, was around at that time. She might be of some help.'

'Well, thanks, Earl. That's something. I have a list of people to talk to—a few I can find and a few I can't.'

'Intriguing, can you share the "can't find" list with me?'

'Love to. There's a woman that visits Tom, or she did until

he threw a beer bottle at her. Name's Carol. Bridget calls her Horsey Carol because she agists a paddock from the Galloways. And now that I've talked to you, I'll love to get a hold of your former driver, he might be the last to see Jean on the day.'

'I'll look into my records, although Prue took care of household staff. But this Horsey Carol, that's got me beat. Sorry. I reckon you'll do well with Iris. She seems to cut everyone's hair. Got a photo of this Carol?'

'No, but Jenna Bragg gave me a bunch of photos she took of Galloway's records and family stuff.'

Earl choked on his coffee. 'Oh good Lord, that one is a trick. Keeps the teachers hopping. Must take after her father.'

'Hmm. Bossy little madam. But switched on–she transferred the images to my computer from her phone while I was calling out for the tech guy. She has all the confidence Bridget lacks.'

'Well, you'll enjoy it when she works there, Peter.' Earl grinned.

'Dear god, no. What do you mean by that?'

'Says she wants to be a policeman.'

'Arrrgh. Shoot me now. She'll turn the place upside down.'

Earl merely wiggled his eyebrows in an altogether superior fashion, but then redeemed his teasing by slyly paying for their meals.

Peter Benson took his leave of Earl, walked along the shoreline. He needed information. Information that would connect Galloway to the body in the scrubland and so far he had nothing.

If it wasn't Jean Galloway, then who the hell was it? And where was Jean Galloway?

By the time Peter Benson had secured a time with Iris Tesler, Byron Galloway had been charged with possession of an illegal amount of marijuana. Benson had been able to persuade Byron that it was in his best interests to cooperate, not only with his possession charges but a murder investigation. Byron consented to a DNA test.

Now it was just a waiting game until the DNA reports returned.

A good time to walk the Galloway property. It was a crime scene now. Tom Galloway was staying in the local hotel after the fire, so he wouldn't be a hindrance.

Benson wasn't expecting to find anything. What would there be on scorched earth?

The firemen had worked on the house until they realised they couldn't save it and the grassy paddocks were a greater threat. A grass fire in this kind of heat could spread wildly. Trees lined the fences. Benson wandered to the end of the property. The grass was brown and lifeless, crunching under his boots. A single crow circled. There was an old, stained bathtub, now nearly empty. The feed bins were full. His keen eye noticed a white piece of paper. He stretched to pick it up. It was a business card. Carol Merchant, Massage & Rehabilitation Therapist. Accredited. 54 Junction Road, Norwood. A mobile phone number.

Benson flicked the card. 'Gotcha.'

Found

Sgt. Peter Benson didn't expect a Japanese garden with a Koi fish pond, set in a courtyard of a well-kept home.

Wearing casual gear, he introduced himself. He'd used his own name, gambling on Carol being unaware of his position. She welcomed him warmly and showed him into the separate section of the house clearly dedicated to her massage work.

Carol fussed with towels and a heating unit. Peter sat down and flipped open his police identification card and badge. He waited for Carol to turn towards him so he could study her reaction.

Carol dropped a metal pair of tongs used for the hot towels. 'You're a policeman. Oh dear. Who died? An accident. What? Officer please tell me. Come in to the lounge room. Can I make you a cup of tea? I'll need one it seems. It's not my brother, is it?'

'No, no. It's about the Galloways.'

Carol put her hand over her mouth and turned to a chair

in the corner where another woman sat.

The woman tried to speak. One side of her face had drooped. She clutched a four prong walking stick and slowly rose to her feet with Carol's help, then shaking Carol off, she crossed the room awkwardly, dragging one foot, then the other. A small section of her hair was missing. Benson had to stop himself from reacting.

As the woman drew near he realised that she had once been beautiful.

She reached out a slim white hand for Benson to shake and softly said, 'I'm Jean Galloway.' The woman grasping his hand and rasped, 'How are my children?'

They sat knee to knee in straight backed chairs near the Koi pond. Peter told her what he could, encouraging her grip on his hand. Jean fought tears, desiring his story of events, his knowledge of the children she'd been unable to see, to know.

The one question that had plagued Peter in all his scenarios of Jean's location was 'how could she stay away?' but seeing her scars and the decimation of her once young slim body, his question was answered.

When he had finished, he hesitated, held both of her hands and asked for her story, the story of the roadside, the leaving, all those years ago.

'I was waiting by the side of the road, hidden by the grevilleas. I'd been as quiet as a mouse. Didn't dare to eat breakfast. It was a crisp, chilly morning. I was going to leave Tom. Take the kids. He had thrashed me a week or so before. I'd stood up to him for the first time. I held a chair up to stop him and said, "I will leave you one day. I will." He was remorseful the next day, giving all the old promises. I was so used to those, and his tears, his groveling for forgiveness. Things went well for a while. He brought flowers home. And I waited. Waited till he was blind drunk one night to pack. He was supposed to be out all day. Some expo. I left early in the morning. Before sunrise. I couldn't take the kids then. The noise, you know. I was going to collect them when they arrived at school.'

Jean paused to wipe her drooping lip. 'The fog was low and thick that day. A flashy black car passed. Someone waved. And I waited for the taxi. Waited for freedom. I could hear my heart in my throat. My stomach was churning. I hadn't eaten much for days, planning, waiting. Tom had been snoring like a chainsaw when I slipped from the bedroom and crept from the house. By the roadside, I waited.'

'I heard a rustling of the grevilleas, thought it might be birds, hoped it might be birds, anything but Tom.'

'Then everything went black, black as a moonless night.'

'I came to with a mouthful of soggy, mouldy leaves and earth. My head was spinning. Tom? Where was he?'

'He'd left me there. Covered in underbrush, leaves and earth. But he was gone and I was alive. That was all that mattered.'

'I fought to get free and through the barbed wire fence. My face was sticky, wet.'

'The world was sideways, tilted off-course, but I ran. Or I think I did. Crooked, strange, slow steps. Frantic steps. Tom might come back, see me, but I stood in the middle of the road, waving manically. I must have looked like Frankenstein. Would anyone stop?'

'The flashy black car came back. A guy in a suit jumped out, said he was ex-military, an employee of the Wainwrights and that he'd come to save me. He talked to me to keep me awake as he drove to the hospital. I'd been screaming in fear, refusing to let him call an ambulance. He took the Onkaparinga Road through Happy Valley down to Flinders Hospital. Far enough from the Noarlunga Hospital so that it wasn't the first place anyone would look for me. After he dropped me off he disappeared. Never knew his name.'

'While I was in hospital I lived in fear. I thought for sure Tom would realise what had happened. That he'd go back and see that I wasn't under the brush. At the hospital I told the staff my husband was overseas and already knew where I was. I told them a water container had fallen on my head, one of those metal mesh things. It was the best I could think of at the time.'

'I met Carol there. She was the rehab therapist. We became close. We've been together ever since.' Carol put an arm on Jean's shoulder.

'Carol offered to look in on the children so she came up with the ruse of having a horse there.'

Carol laughed. 'How hard that has been. I'm rubbish with horses. It was my brother's horse. He was none too pleased with the idea, but when he met my darling Jean, well, it was another matter. He saw how happy I was, how happy we were. And how Jean had suffered.' Carol handed Jean a handkerchief for the torrent of tears falling at the end of the story. Carol kissed her forehead. 'I took photos whenever I could. I had to be so careful. We knew Tom wouldn't file a Missing Person's report, wouldn't put photos on electric poles or shop windows.

Sorry, I get emotional. The only thing keeping Jean safe was the fact that old bastard thought she was dead.'

Jean still gripped Peter Benson's hands. She saw the traces of tears in his eyes. She knew that his relentless efforts had brought the truth to light, opened a door for her.

'Please, Sergeant. Can you bring my children to me? They would be protected with you.' She wiped her eyes. 'But only when it's safe, you hear? When you know that Tom will be locked up for a very long time.'

'Or dead,' said Carol, then covered her mouth.

The motherless ones

If anyone had asked Peter Benson to describe his type of woman, he'd have said, 'any sort', that is, until he met Iris Tesler.

It was a punch in the gut to see her for the first time, standing in the courtyard behind her shop, where the walls were old stone and ivy covered a well. There was a rustic iron staircase on the outside of the house. Iris wore a circular Spanish skirt and red shoes as if she had been in the middle of a salsa or tango. Her dark hair was held up loosely with a colourful scarf.

She was humming and vainly trying to put seed in a bird feeder up high in a native frangipani tree that had spilled its delicious fragrance everywhere.

'That tree gets bigger every year,' she told him as he approached. 'But that doesn't bother me as much as the neighbours. Fussy buggers. Anyway, you must be Sergeant Peter Benson, aka The Pink Panther.'

Peter laughed. The first gut-busting chuckle in recent

history.

Iris tilted her head and smiled cheekily. 'I do hope you're more sure-footed than Inspector Clouseau. I can't reach the bird feeder.'

So Peter Benson reached up and put bird seed in a bird feeder for the first time in his life. And then he forgot why he'd come. He had met Carol. Tick. And Jean—an unexpected delight. Tick. And the other things? Never mind, they would come to him. Sooner or later.

'I can see why you're a sought after hairdresser, you have such gorgeous hair.'

'Why thank you, kind sir. It's my best wig, cost a fortune.' She tossed her hair back, then seeing Peter's stunned look, added, 'I'm kidding, Clouseau.' Iris moved towards an outdoor setting, reaching for a chair.

'Oh, I'll get you for that.' Peter felt the tension of the past weeks seeping from his body. He couldn't get enough of the woman sitting opposite. He hoped he wasn't staring like a teenage boy, but wow. How strange and irrational a thing attraction is, a chemical reaction to another human being.

Iris brushed dust off the table and sighed. 'I'll tell you what I can.'

Peter noted that even in a serious mood, Iris was stunning.

'I can tell you about the motherless ones,' she said.

'The motherless ones?' Peter's forehead wrinkled. He waited.

'That trio, Jenna, Ebony and Bridget. They are so different but they fit together like hands in gloves. Jenna and Ebony got together first. They were both the new kids. You know how that is. No one wants to talk to you. Not in high school. So they teamed up naturally. Of course, the addition of Bridget is not as easily understood. Unless you know their stories.'

'Go on.'

'Ebony grew up to her teens without a mother and the yawning cavern of not knowing why she died, whether it was suicide or an accident. So she had those years. Empty. Being the woman of the house. I don't blame Brady. He was drowning in grief and confusion himself. Then Emma came along—I should tell you that I'm her mother. Ebony loves Emma and they get along, but it takes compromise for both of them. And Jenna, her mother has been in and out of her life for most of her life. Jenna's been sent back and forth to Jack like a library book. Her mother is an actor, no domestic skills or interest, so Jenna took over.'

'Ah, that makes sense—she's a firecracker.'

'You've met then,' laughed Iris.

'And Bridget, naturally motherless for those preteen and teen years, being the woman of the house, cooking etc. But defeated, sullen and silent. She's doing better with Leah, basically her mother substitute. I do hope you can solve some of this mess.'

'Oh. I forgot to tell you. I found Jean.'

'Jean! Jean Galloway? My best friend from school.'

Between the weeping and demanding to see her friend *immediately*, Peter learned that Jean had been a foster child, one broken and abused by the system. Just the type for a predator to possess and abuse.

Peter told her of the Koi pond, the lovely home, and then Jean's scars and disability. Lastly the love she found with Carol.

'Oh my, that'll be a lot for those kids to take in.'

Peter's phone beeped. The DNA results were in. There was no match with Bridget or Byron. However, the woman had been pregnant at the time of her murder and the foetus was a match to the two siblings.

The connection he needed.

'Work?' asked Iris.

'Yes, sorry.' Peter stood and pushed his chair in.

'Bye. See you, Clouseau.'

'Absolutely you will, Iris Tesler.'

Saying nothing

Tom Galloway didn't like his second visit to the police station any more than the first. 'Thought you lot liked to do home visits,' he laughed, his gait was awkward, even though he was held up by two officers. 'Ah. Fffricking hell, ya bought me here fer a ressst when I was quite capable of getting sssome kip at th'hotel without you fine gentlemens ssshtinking company.'

Benson decided not to argue the finer points of the meaning of arrest as opposed to a rest, telling the constable to tuck him up nice and sweet in their superior accommodations. Then he called a doctor to attend to the old guy. He didn't want anything going wrong with this chance. He couldn't let Tom Galloway back on the street.

He sat at his desk, twirling a pencil as he planned his interview once Galloway was part-way to sober. Not stone cold sober, otherwise he'd have to deal with the delirium tremens, and if he had a hysterical man with seizures he'd have to admit him to the hospital, which he would probably have to do at some stage. He'd also noticed Galloway's yellow eyes, his deep wheezing cough, and by his gait that hip surgery hadn't gone so well. No, sooner was better than later.

Peter Benson wanted information and he had a hunch.

'So, how'd you meet Shirl, Tom?'

'Where'd you think I met chicksss? At church? Ha ha! I'm not talking about Ssshirl Davis to you. Nobody wanted her. No one, 'cept me. I was the only one to pay her any mind. She thrived wi' me.' Galloway poked the table emphatically with his right forefinger. 'Right firecracker, that one. No matter how many times she got kicked outta the pub for being underage, she'd come right back. To me. That'sh gumption, that.'

'Interview concluded...' Benson stood.

Tom Galloway thumped the table. 'I ain't done sssaying nothin' yet.'

Benson ordered Galloway back to the cells then organised custody in the local detox. Speaking to the other officers, he said, 'Galloway talked like a parrot. Not a confession as such, but close. We'll have another go at him when he's sober and fit to make a formal statement. But it's good news fellas. We have an ID on the body.

A mother

No words or images, explanations or descriptions could have prepared Bridget to meet her mother. Ten long years, longer then she had known Jean as a mother.

Benson had had to stop twice for the anxious girl to dry retch beside the car. Too much, too much. A father arrested, a brother on his way to mandated rehabilitation, and a daughter lost and disconnected.

If only Jean had remained seated, instead of the slow jerking advance, swinging from side to side, punching the ground with that four pronged stick thing. With her half frozen face and Halloween smile. A stranger, a grotesque one at that.

Jean held a handkerchief to her lips to pat the moist dampness of one side of her mouth. 'The stroke,' she said, her voice strained.

Bridget had been unable to replace the image she'd had as a six year old child, of her bright smiling mother. The one in the photograph she'd been keeping on her phone since Jenna had found it. This was so far from the mother she'd known, now with dirty blonde hair, so lacking the shine of the past, short with a patch missing. For a teen whose only experience with modernity and life had been through two other motherless teens, Bridget was cast adrift.

Seeing her daughter's grim fearful face, Jean paused. Then shuffled back to the recliner in the courtyard.

Byron frolicked up to his mother like a jubilant puppy, easing the tense silence emanating from Bridget.

'Jeez, Mum, sorry, um, heck. That bastard, did this to you.' He patted her hair gingerly. 'I'll murder the old dude.'

Benson jangled his coffee cup, frowned at Byron, who studiously ignored him. Byron didn't want to offend the policeman. He might spill the beans on Byron's upcoming treatment appointment. Their mother didn't need to know that particular detail. Not now.

'Y'need a manicure, Mum,' said Byron, turning his mother's good hand over, revealing multi-coloured specks.

Jean laughed, as natural a sound as Bridget had ever heard, striking memories, faint yet true.

'Not much cause for that, Byron. Not when I use my fingers to mix and paint.'

Bridget looked at her own hands. 'Do you still do that, Mum?'

'I do,' said Jean, tilting her head forward hopefully. 'You helped me paint the sunflower sign for the garden. Remember?'

'Yes.' Bridget spoke, but only a whisper, for their father had razed the garden low and burnt Jean's stakes and signs, and worse still, that was now the burial place for the kitten she had cherished.

'I have some albums of photos that Carol took. When ... if ... next time.' Jean pointed to some bound albums on a bookshelf. 'I know today is a short visit. Thank you for bringing them Sergeant.'

Sergeant Peter Benson was wearing his uniform because they were taking Byron to the Salvation Army drug rehab centre in the city. Byron would be there six weeks. This visit to Jean and Carol was a courtesy stop on the way. One that could be explained later.

'It's no trouble Jean. Iris Tesler sends her best.'

'And ... him ... Tom?'

'He's locked up, awaiting trial. However I must tell you that he has liver failure and emphysema. He's in the prison hospital. Lucky to have six months. He's not a young man, so you should be prepared.'

There was silence for a minute.

Byron stared at the ceiling. He hadn't registered the last few sentences. His six week rehabilitation was weighing on his mind. He had visions of being toothless like Benji. 'Destruction everywhere, Mum. Dad got rid of all of it,' he said, linking his hands behind his head. 'Pyromaniac. Burnt the whole damn house down, Mum.'

Peter Benson raised an eyebrow. This kid was veering all over the place. Nervous. Good. That meant rehab might do some good.

'Sheds as well?' asked Jean.

'Nah, missed those. Too drunk.'

'Then check the large barrel at the back of the big shed. The one with the lid.'

'Righto.'

'Don't forget, Byron.'

'No, Mum.'

Byron was chatting with his mother as if it was only a few days since he'd seen her and the effect on Bridget was unsettling.

The more she heard her mother's voice, the more the memories started trickling back. She'd expected instant recognition, but realised that had been foolish. Even if their mother hadn't been scarred and deformed from the attack, she'd have been older, different. And Bridget had only been six, relying on rosy dreams, ribbons and lace, balloons and butterflies.

Peter Benson cleared his throat. 'We must go. I'm sorry.'

Byron nodded, kissed his mother's head.

Jean tugged on Carol's sleeve. 'Give Bridgee some sweet drink, will you love. Otherwise she'll faint. Sprite still a favourite, Bridgee?'

Bridget nodded. 'Did I faint when I was a kid, Mum?'

'Over like nine pins at the bowling alley. Down you'd go without a hint. Does it still happen, darling?'

Bridget flushed. 'Sometimes.'

'Right bloody nuisance, she is,' said Byron, rubbing Bridget's head until she thumped him.

It was the most normal moment of the visit.

As soon as the door clicked shut Jean crumpled. 'She hates me.' Jean crumpled in the chair. 'How can I blame her? I have no words to help her understand. Maybe I should have gone to the police, told my story...' She wept.

'Oh Jean it was two years before you could walk again.'

'And only because of you Carol. What did I do to deserve such love? If you could love a cripple, maybe one day, she will. I'm a stranger, an ugly stranger.'

'Not to me, never to me. She just needs time, Jean,' said Carol, kissing the tears on Jean's cheek. 'She hated me for years.'

'Well, that's no surprise with your driving, darling.'

Bridget idly kicked stones down the driveway to the car.

'You could've tried, Bridgee.' Byron ruffled his sister's hair. 'She's still our mother. You could've tried.'

'I fucken did. What would you know? You weren't the one getting belted by Da every time he was drunk, or not drunk, just gnarly.'

'Why do you think I left home at fifteen, staying on a couch here, an outbuilding there? Sometimes sneaking into my own bed for a few hours, wondering why your door was locked.'

'Why do you think? That studded belt hanging by the back door wasn't there to keep his trousers up.'

'Oh Bridgee. God, I'm sorry. You too? I never knew. I thought you were the adored favourite. Da always introduced you as his princess.'

'I wasn't his princess when no one was there. I was nothing, worse than nothing, *nothing* gets ignored, *nothing* doesn't get beaten, *nothing* is a shadow. You wanna know what they call me at school? Shadow Girl.' Bridget shoved him away, fighting tears. Her father's words, haunting—*Don't cry, Don't cry. I'll give yer somethin' to cry about.*

Byron was silent in the car on the way to the rehab centre. The reality of his situation had hit home. Hard.

At the centre, in the carpark, Benson flipped the boot, retrieved Byron's backpack and thumped him on the back. 'Don't waste a minute of your time here kid. You only want to come once. And you will if you're as smart as I think you are.'

As Bridget saw her brother's defeated shoulders, his dragging steps, she burst from the car, ran to him and hugged him, bawling like a newborn babe. 'Oh Byron. I'm sorry. Please get better. I nearly died when you were in hospital.'

'S'okay Bridgee. I promise.' Byron held her awkwardly and kissed the top of her head, his backpack slipping to the ground.

Benson opened the passenger door, silently inviting Bridget to sit in the front. The floodgates of weeping had opened. Bridget couldn't stop crying.

Benson handed her a handkerchief. 'Always prepared,' he said.

'Get many cry-babies in your job?' Bridget sniffled.

'You wouldn't believe how many people cry in front of cops,' Benson said, shaking his head.

'What? Even the men?'

'Oh yeah. Always the men. 'Specially if they're guilty. Regular garden sprinklers they are then.' Benson stole a glance. Bridget's face was thoughtful, working herself up to a question.

Experience told him that, so he waited.

'Did you find out about the woman? The, um, one in the scrub, y'know, on our land.'

'Her name was Shirley Davis. She ran away from home when she was fifteen. A wild child. Fed up with the rules at home. Ran away a lot apparently. Not every fifteen year old ends up on the news as a Missing Person. People don't realise that. She usually ran away with some dope-headed boy who owned a car. That's what she did the last time. Came from Sydney. Then the boy dumped her. She hung out in the bars and hotels. Slept on the beach. Met your father. Moved in with him. He must've freaked when he found out she was pregnant. Hit her with…'

'Pregnant? She was a pregnant teen?'

'Yeah. That's the way we caught your father out. DNA. The baby was his.'

'What sort?'

'Sort?'

'Boy or girl.'

'Oh right. Girl.'

'Fuck. Oh. Sorry.'

'Don't be sorry. I think you've earned the right to say fuck for a long time yet.'

'How did he…?'

'He hit her with a crowbar.'

'The one hanging in the shed?'

'Yeah. That was the one.'

'He just left it there? Oh dear God.'

'It had some of your mother's hair and skin as well as

Shirl's. Look if this is too much Bridget ... It's just that it'll all be in the newspaper. Probably is already.'

'So Mum, he hit her with it and ... she got away somehow...'

Peter Benson took a deep breath and then told Bridget what he'd already told Byron, had told Iris and had written in a long report that made him wish he could cry the whole way through the writing and the telling.

He told Bridget of her mother's burial in the low, mossy sludge of the scrubland, her fighting to survive, to live, although concussed and bleeding. How all she could think about was two children who needed her. Of her mother's years of terrified hiding in plain sight, only safe while Tom Galloway thought her dead.

He told her that the officers had already found the suitcase, hidden in the barrel. How it held clothes for her children, train tickets for three, toys for the long journey to Byron Bay.

He didn't tell her of his phone call with the parents of Shirley Davis. The gutted mother and father of a wayward girl and her grotesque end.

'Can we stop on the way back?' Bridget asked.

Bridget rushed through the door, kissed her mother on both cheeks, wet from recent tears, blended with tears of her own.

'You remember me, Bridgee?'

'I remember, Mamma. I love you still. I love you again. I love you for always.'